Contents

The Lost of Ridgefield	1
Katrina Case	2
Prologue	4
Chapter One: The Last Night of Freedom	9
Chapter Two: The Consequences of Defiance	13
Chapter Three: The Walls Close	18
Chapter Four: A Smile That Wasn't a Lie	23
Chapter Five: The Night the Door Closed	30
Chapter Six: The First Day at Ridgefield	35
Chapter Seven: The Doctor's Diagnosis The Aldridge Estate	40
Chapter Eight: The Weight of Betrayal	45
Chapter Nine: A Prison of Their Making	50
Chapter Eleven: Shattered Composure	55
Chapter Twelve: Fractured Bonds	60
Chapter Thirteen: Unraveling Truths	65
Chapter Fourteen: Fractured Realities	70
Chapter Fifteen: A Mind Unraveling	75

Chapter Sixteen: Beneath the Surface	80
Chapter Seventeen: Shadows of the Past	86
Chapter Eighteen: Shattered Minds and Silent Rebellion	91
Chapter Nineteen: A Reckoning at Dawn	96
Chapter Twenty: Fractured Paths and Desperate Salvation	101
Chapter Twenty-One: Shadows of Freedom	108
Chapter Twenty-Two: A Fading Light and a Rising Storm	114
Chapter Twenty-Three: Fragments of Truth and Unfinished Battles	119
Chapter Twenty-Four: Between Fear and Fate	127
Chapter Twenty-Five: A House of Ruin and a Fractured Mind	135
Chapter Twenty-Six: Shadows of the Past	143
Chapter Twenty-Seven: A House of Silence and a City of Secrets	151
Chapter Twenty-Eight: The Weight of Names	159
Chapter Twenty-Nine: Shadows of the Past	165
Chapter Thirty: Beneath the Surface	173
Chapter Thirty-One: A Sin to Be Silenced	177
Chapter Thirty-Two: A Choice of Power and Love	184
Chapter Thirty-Three: Bound by Vows, Driven by Purpose	190
Chapter Thirty-Five: The Vanishing	198
Chapter Thirty-Six: The Trap is Set	203

March 1856

Chapter Thirty-Seven: Into the Lion's Den   211
March 6, 1856 – The Taylor Estate

Chapter Thirty-Eight: Fractured Truths   218

Chapter Thirty-Nine: A Grave Conversation   224

Chapter Forty: The Breaking Point   228

Chapter Forty-One: A New Beginning   234

Chapter Forty-Two: A Future Reclaimed   239

The Lost of Ridgefield

Katrina Case

The Lost of Ridgefield
Copyright © 2025 Katrina Case

All rights reserved. No part of this book may be reproduced, stored in a retrieval system, or transmitted in any form or by any means—electronic, mechanical, photocopying, recording, or otherwise—without prior written permission from the publisher, except for brief quotations in reviews or academic purposes.

This is a work of fiction. Names, characters, places, and incidents are products of the author's imagination or are used fictitiously. Any resemblance to actual persons, living or dead, events, or locales is entirely coincidental.

Literary Reflections
ISBN: 979-8-89766-751-2

For permissions, inquiries, or more information, contact: https://literaryreflections.com

Prologue

Boston, Massachusetts – February 1856

The house was silent, except for the rhythmic ticking of the grandfather clock in the parlor and the occasional crackle of the dying embers in the hearth. Outside, a heavy mist rolled in from the harbor, swallowing the gas-lit streets in a dense, ghostly veil. The city slept, unaware of the betrayal unfolding within the walls of the Taylor residence.

Reginald Taylor moved through the dimly lit hallway, his polished shoes barely making a sound against the gleaming hardwood floors. His expression remained unreadable, his hands tucked behind his back as he paused near the rear entrance right on time. He reached for the latch, his movements measured and deliberate, and pulled the door open.

Two men stepped inside, their heavy coats still damp from the night air. Neither spoke nor did they need to. Reginald had given his instructions earlier that day, and these men were well-versed in their duties. They removed their hats, nodding in silent acknowledgment before turning toward the staircase.

Margaret Taylor stood at the edge of the parlor, her silk nightgown pooling at her feet. A single candle flickered on the side table beside her, casting soft shadows along her delicate features. Tears glistened in her eyes, but she did not step forward. She had agreed to this. It was for the best.

Still, when her husband met her gaze, she could not hold it. With a sharp inhale, she turned away, her hands trembling as she clutched the delicate lace of her nightgown.

The men ascended the staircase with slow, deliberate steps. The house was still, but the weight of what would happen pressed down like a heavy fog.

Katherine's bedroom door stood slightly ajar, the soft glow of a dying oil lamp flickering within. Inside, she lay curled beneath the covers, her golden hair spilling over the pillow in tangled waves. She looked peaceful—the last moment of peace she would know for a very long time.

The first man moved swiftly, stepping beside the bed and clamping a rough hand over her mouth before she could stir. The other reached for her arms, pinning them to the mattress as she jolted awake. A muffled scream tore from her throat, her body thrashing violently beneath their grasp. Panic flooded her senses, her heart slamming against her ribs as she struggled against the unseen force dragging her from sleep.

"No!" she choked, her words swallowed by the cloth pressed tightly over her mouth. "No, please!"

She kicked, twisted—fought. But they were stronger.

The damp fabric in their hands reeked of something sickly sweet, and the moment the scent hit her lungs, the fight began to slip from her limbs. A haze crept over her vision, her frantic movements slowing as the drug took hold.

Just before the darkness claimed her, she saw movement in the doorway, a shadowed figure watching.

"Mother…" The whisper barely left her lips before her body slumped, the last of her strength fading into nothing.

Margaret did not move. She did not reach for her daughter.

She turned away.

The sharp jolt of carriage wheels rattling over uneven roads pulled Katherine from unconsciousness. Cold air seeped through the cracks in the wooden frame, biting against her skin, and when she opened her eyes, she realized she was bound. Her wrists were secured with thick restraints, the coarse material digging into her flesh.

Her mind spun, confusion warring with panic as she struggled to remember.

Then it came crashing back.

The hands. The struggle. The cloth pressed against her face.

Her mother was standing in the doorway, watching as she was taken.

A choked sob tore from her throat as she twisted against the bindings, but the effort was futile. Across from her sat the two men, their faces expressionless as they watched her without concern. She was nothing more than a task to complete, another body to deliver.

"Why?" The word left her in a strangled gasp. "Why are you doing this? Why is this happening?"

The men did not answer. They didn't even blink.

Katherine turned her head toward the minor, glass-paned window, her breath catching as she saw where they were taking her.

Beyond the thick fog, a massive stone structure loomed in the darkness, its shadow stretching across the land like a waiting beast. The iron gates stood open, their intricate design twisted and jagged, and countless windows lined the towering building beyond them. Most were dark and lifeless, but one, high above, glowed faintly against the night.

The carriage rattled to a stop, and the doors were thrown open.

"No!" Katherine's breath came in short, panicked gasps as rough hands seized her, dragging her from the carriage with brutal efficiency. Her feet barely touched the gravel path before she was pulled toward the looming entrance. The doors, impossibly tall and arched, creaked open before her.

She stumbled, her body still weak from the sedative, but they did not slow.

Her terror built with every step. "Please, let me go! You don't understand!"

She pleaded, her voice breaking, but her words fell into the void, unheard.

A grand, dimly lit corridor stretched before her, lined with towering bookshelves and heavy oak doors. The scent of burning oil and something metallic lingered in the air. The walls seemed to breathe, as if the building was alive, swallowing her whole.

A figure stepped forward.

Nurse Mary-Alice Alexander.

Her face was gentle, her brown eyes filled with something almost like pity. She placed a steady hand on Katherine's arm, her grip firm but not cruel.

"You're safe now," she said softly.

Safe. The word was so ridiculous that Katherine might have laughed if she weren't on the verge of hysteria.

"Why?" Her voice broke. "Why am I here?"

Mary-Alice didn't answer.

She couldn't.

Before Katherine could push further, another figure entered the room.

Dr. Julian Aldridge.

His movements were measured, and his pristine white coat contrasted with the dark surroundings. His gaze flickered to the men who had delivered her, and he nodded slightly before dismissing them.

Then, his eyes fell on Katherine.

For the first time that night, the silence in the room shifted—not from the ticking of a clock or the closing of doors, but from something unseen.

Dr. Aldridge's expression remained unreadable, yet his eyes lingered, his head tilting slightly as if examining something familiar, something unsettling.

A flicker of recognition.

The stillness stretched between them, and Katherine, despite her fear, felt it too.

Her chest rose and fell in shallow, panicked breaths. Why was he looking at her like that?

The weight of his stare sent a chill curling up her spine.

She was not another patient to him.

He knew something.

As the doors to Ridgefield sealed shut behind her, Katherine realized that whatever fate awaited her had already been decided.

Chapter One: The Last Night of Freedom

The grand ballroom of the Taylor estate shimmered beneath the glow of gilded chandeliers, their crystal prisms casting fractured light across the polished marble floors. The scent of fresh-cut roses and beeswax polish filled the air, mingling with the murmur of polite conversation and the steady hum of waltz music played by a quartet near the towering bay windows.

Katherine Ann Taylor stood at the edge of the room, her gloved hands clasped tightly in front of her waist, fingers twitching against the stiff satin of her gown. The icy blue fabric shimmered beneath the candlelight, the off-the-shoulder sleeves adorned with delicate embroidery, a gift from her mother who had insisted it would make her look more refined—more desirable.

She felt trapped in its perfection.

Her golden-blonde hair, curled into precise ringlets, had been pinned back with pearl combs, though a few rebellious strands had slipped loose at her temples. The weight of a pearl necklace pressed against her collarbone was a reminder of her mother's expectations. But her eyes, a pale blue-gray that shifted with the light, held the truth she dared not speak aloud—resentment, dread, and the aching knowledge that this was all a performance.

Across the room, Reginald Taylor stood near the

grand staircase, his frame tall and severe. He was dressed in a dark tailcoat with silver cufflinks that caught candlelight. His brown eyes, sharp and calculating, swept over the guests, pausing when they landed on her. It was a silent warning: Behave.

Beside him, Margaret Taylor, his wife, remained poised. She was a vision of composed elegance in a deep wine-colored silk gown, her hazel eyes as unreadable as ever. Her dark blonde hair, though streaked with the faintest hints of gray, was styled in an elaborate updo adorned with sapphire pins.

Katherine knew what was coming before her father moved toward her, his polished boots clicking against the floor with quiet authority.

"You are to meet someone," he murmured, barely glancing at her before shifting his gaze toward a man approaching from the far side of the room.

Katherine swallowed hard.

Daniel Hahn was taller than most men in the room, broad-shouldered with perfectly combed chestnut-brown hair and piercing dark eyes that rarely wavered. His strong jawline and straight nose would have made him conventionally handsome, but there was something cold about his expression—calculated, as if every movement was measured. He wore a crisp black evening coat, white waistcoat, and a silver watch chain glinting under the ballroom's golden light.

His father, Alistair Hahn, was close behind him, a man of near-unrivaled wealth and reputation. His graying hair was still thick and neatly parted, and his mouth set in the tight-lipped expression of a man accustomed to getting what he wanted.

Lillian "Lily" Taylor, only nine years old, had been

lingering near their mother but now peered around Margaret's skirts, her large green eyes filled with curiosity and mischief. Her golden-blonde curls, slightly darker than Katherine's, bounced as she fidgeted with the ribbon on her dress, a soft shade of lavender.

She was too young to understand the weight of what was happening, too innocent to see the chains being placed around Katherine's wrists.

Katherine turned back to Daniel, forcing a polite nod as her stomach twisted.

Reginald continued, his tone clipped, efficient. "Daniel, I'd like to introduce my eldest daughter, Katherine formally."

Daniel inclined his head, his gaze assessing her. "Miss Taylor," he said smoothly. "A pleasure, I'm sure."

A pleasure, he's sure.

Katherine wanted to rip the pearls from her throat, to step out of this gown, out of this life, and disappear into the night. Instead, she dipped into a practiced curtsy that her mother had drilled into her since childhood.

Daniel extended his hand, an invitation to dance.

Katherine hesitated.

Then, without another word, she turned and walked away.

The streets of Boston were alive with the hum of late-night carriages, the glow of gas lamps flickering against the damp Cobblestone roads. Katherine's slippers were not made for walking these streets, but she didn't care. She needed to breathe.

The scent of the harbor carried on the wind, mingling with the faint aroma of fresh bread from a nearby bakery closing for the night. She rounded a familiar corner, her pulse slowing when she saw the warm light spilling from a small storefront.

Montgomery & Son Printing Press.

Elias Montgomery stood just outside, sleeves rolled up, arms crossed as he leaned against the doorframe.

His dark hair was slightly tousled, no doubt from a long day's work, and his hazel eyes flickered between amusement and relief when they landed on her. The glow from the streetlamp cast a warm hue over his strong jawline, the shadow of stubble visible in the dim light.

"Katherine?" His voice carried the same ease it always had, but something deeper beneath it was a quiet understanding.

She stopped in front of him, breathless, her heart still racing from the weight of the evening. "Elias."

His lips quirked, though his gaze sharpened as he took her in. "Should I be concerned that you're wandering the city alone at this hour?" He tilted his head, watching her closely. "Or has your father finally decided to set you free?"

A laugh bubbled up, unbidden. "Hardly."

Elias didn't smile this time. Instead, he sighed, running a hand through his hair. "Come inside," he said, stepping aside. "You could use a moment to clear your head."

Katherine hesitated. She should turn back. She should have returned before her father realized she was gone.

But then she thought of Daniel. Of the ballroom. Of the suffocating weight of her future pressing in around her.

Just a moment, she told herself.

And so, she stepped inside.

Chapter Two: The Consequences of Defiance

Once alive with music and polite conversation, the grand halls of the Taylor estate had now fallen into silence. The chandeliers still gleamed above the polished marble floors, their crystals catching the flickering glow of the remaining candlelight. Servants moved quietly through the space, clearing away the remnants of the evening's grand affair—half-empty champagne flutes, crumpled linen napkins, abandoned plates still dusted with sugared confections.

Katherine had returned through the servant's entrance, her pulse still unsteady from the hurried walk back from Elias' shop. The rich scent of wax-polished wood and fading floral arrangements lingered in the air, cloying and suffocating after the crisp openness of the night. She had hoped—naively, perhaps—that she might slip past unnoticed.

But as she stepped further into the hall, she realized her hope had been in vain.

A presence loomed in the dim candlelight.

"Katherine Ann Taylor."

Reginald Taylor's voice, though never raised, carried the same weight as a blade pressed against the throat. He stood at the base of the grand staircase, hands clasped behind his back, his posture rigid with disapproval. The fine cut of his midnight-black tailcoat only enhanced the severity of his frame, his sharp brown eyes—so unlike her own—glinting beneath the heavy brows that had furrowed in displeasure.

Behind him, Margaret Taylor stood with her arms loosely folded, the rich wine-colored silk of her gown shimmering in the low light. Her hazel eyes, so often unreadable, flickered with something unreadable, concern perhaps, or simply exhaustion.

Katherine swallowed against the tightness in her throat. She would not cower. She had already lost so much of herself in this house—she would not easily offer up the rest.

She lifted her chin. "Father."

Reginald's gaze swept over her—a silent inventory, a dissection of her disobedience. The faint trace of windblown hair at her temples, the slightly creased fabric of her gown, the flush still high on her cheeks from the cool air outside.

"You left the party," he said, each word crisp and clipped, stripped of warmth.

Katherine forced her spine straight, though the weight of his scrutiny threatened to crush her beneath it. "Yes."

"You disrespected not only this family but our guests," he continued, his expression unreadable. "Daniel Hahn and his father in particular."

At the mention of Daniel, a bitter taste settled on Katherine's tongue.

Without needing to ask, she knew that Daniel had noticed her absence. And more importantly—so had Charles Hahn. A man like Daniel's father, a merchant king of industry, would not tolerate a slight, not even an unspoken one.

    Katherine's fingers curled into her skirts, the delicate blue satin crumpling beneath her touch. "Daniel Hahn is not my concern."

    Her father's lips pressed into a thin line. "He is if I say he is."

    Something profound in Katherine's chest tightened. Reginald Taylor had always commanded his world with unwavering precision. He demanded respect, shaped fortunes with a single investment, and ruined men with the flick of a quill. But Katherine was not a business transaction to be arranged at his will.

    And yet, as she stood before him, she felt like one.

    "I will not be forced into marriage with a man I do not love," she said, her voice firm despite the tremor in her fingers.

    Reginald inhaled slowly, his gaze unreadable. "You speak as though your wishes are of any consequence in this matter."

    The finality in his voice struck her like a blow.

    A tense silence stretched between them, thick and suffocating.

    Reginald stepped forward, his polished boots clicking softly against the floor. "Daniel Hahn is a man of wealth, intelligence, and ambition. He would provide you a comfortable life, free of hardship and disgrace." He tilted his head slightly as though observing a flawed sculpture, one in need of reshaping. "It is far more than you deserve after tonight's spectacle."

    Katherine's chest burned with a tangled mix of anger and despair. "And if I refuse?"

    Her father studied her for a long moment, then exhaled as if her disobedience had exhausted him. It had not angered him—it had disappointed him. That was worse.

"Then I will ensure that you have no choices left."

The candlelight flickered, its glow casting deep shadows against the grand columns and gilded moldings. The room suddenly felt smaller, suffocating, as though the walls were closing.

Katherine turned to her mother then, her last, desperate attempt at salvation.

Margaret Taylor had always been a quiet woman—elegant, refined, ever the picture of what society expected. But Katherine had once hoped, perhaps foolishly, that there was more beneath the surface. That beneath the cool detachment, beneath the carefully measured words, her mother might—just once—choose her over the life that had been carved out for them.

She met her mother's gaze, silently pleading.

Margaret held her stare for only a moment, her chest rising in a measured breath. Then, with careful precision, she looked away.

Katherine's stomach twisted.

A small hand gripped the fabric of Katherine's gown, and she startled at the touch.

Lillian.

The little girl had crept from the staircase unnoticed, her wide green eyes darting between their parents and Katherine, confusion written plainly across her face. She clutched at the fabric of her dress, the slight tremble of her hands betraying her unease.

"Katie?" Lily's voice was soft, uncertain.

Katherine turned instinctively, placing a hand against her sister's curls, smoothing them down in what she hoped was a reassuring gesture. "It's alright, Lily," she murmured.

Reginald sighed, long and slow. "Lillian, return to bed. This is not a matter that concerns you."

Lily hesitated, glancing back up at Katherine. Katherine had always been her protector, whispering stories to her at night, brushing the tangles from her curls in the morning, and holding her when their father's words were sharp and unrelenting.

But tonight, Katherine could not protect her.

Tonight, Katherine could barely protect herself.

Lily's lip trembled but obeyed, stepping back and disappearing up the staircase.

Reginald turned his attention back to Katherine, his expression carefully measured as though deciding what piece to move next in his silent game of chess.

"You will marry Daniel Hahn," he said. His voice was calm, almost gentle, but Katherine knew better. It was not kindness. It was a certainty.

Katherine felt something inside her crack, splintering like ice under pressure.

She had walked into a trap.

Reginald had never intended to ask. He had only been waiting for an excuse.

And now, she had given him one.

Chapter Three: The Walls Close

The Taylor estate had never felt like home, but now, it felt like a gilded prison. Five days had passed since the night of the party, and Katherine's world grew smaller with each sunrise. At first, there had been a subtle new expectation that she would not leave the house without a chaperone, servants hovering a little too closely, and her father's watchful eye lingering longer than usual.

But then, she noticed the actual changes.

Her letters never seemed to reach their recipients. She had written to Elias once, but just a short note slipped into the hands of a trusted maid. By morning, it had mysteriously vanished. The staff, always polite, now carried an unspoken tension in their movements, as if they were afraid of something.

Even the estate gates, once open during the day for visitors and deliveries, were now closed at all hours.

She had been locked inside without ever hearing the key turn.

The morning sun filtered weakly through the lace curtains of the breakfast room, casting pale golden streaks across the long mahogany table. The air smelled of fresh rolls, butter, and tea—warm and familiar, yet it churned Katherine's stomach.

Her mother sat across from her, as composed as ever. Her gloved hands rested gently in her lap, and a small spoon meticulously stirred her tea.

Margaret Taylor looked at ease, but Katherine knew better.

"Father is arranging the engagement," Katherine said, watching closely for a reaction.

Margaret's gaze flickered upward but revealed nothing. "You knew this was coming, Katherine." Her fingers tightened around the edge of the table. "I never agreed to it."

Margaret exhaled softly, setting her spoon down with a quiet clink against the porcelain saucer. "No one is asking for your agreement."

The words landed like a blow.

Katherine swallowed hard, her heartbeat rising. "You don't have to let him do this," she said, lowering her voice. "You could speak to him, convince him that I—"

Margaret let out a soft, humorless laugh. "Convince him? You misunderstand your father, my dear. He has already made his decision. And you will do as is expected."

Katherine's breath caught in her throat.

Her mother had never been unkind, not in the way her father was, but she had never been an ally, either. She existed in the space between—a silent observer, a woman who had long since surrendered to the life her husband dictated.

Katherine had always told herself she would never become her mother.

But now, she was beginning to wonder if she had a choice.

The sound of footsteps in the hall made her turn sharply.

Reginald Taylor entered the room with the same controlled confidence he carried in all things. His dark morning coat was buttoned neatly, his silver pocket watch glinting in the light as he moved toward his seat. He initially did not acknowledge Katherine, pouring himself a cup of coffee with slow, measured movements.

Only once he had taken a sip did he look up.

"Daniel Hahn will be calling this afternoon."

Katherine's stomach clenched.

"You will meet with him," Reginald continued, setting his cup down. "And you will behave appropriately."

The unspoken *or else* lingered in the air between them.

Katherine forced herself to breathe evenly. "And if I refuse?"

Reginald met her gaze with something cold, immovable. "You won't."

She wanted to argue, to rise from her seat and slam her hands against the table to demand her freedom. But what good would that do?

Every move she made, every resistance, only tightened the noose.

Later that afternoon, Lily found her in the library.

The girl had snuck away from her bedroom, her curls bouncing as she tiptoed across the rug with the grace of someone who had done it many times before.

"Katie," she whispered, sitting on the chaise beside her. Her large green eyes were wide with concern.

Katherine sighed, setting aside the book she hadn't been reading. "You shouldn't be in here, Lily."

Lily hesitated, twisting the fabric of her lavender dress between her fingers. "Is it true? About you and Mr. Hahn?"

Katherine's throat tightened. "Who told you that?"

"I heard Father talking about it," Lily admitted, shifting closer. "He said it's already arranged."

Katherine's hands curled into fists.

"It isn't fair," Lily said, her voice small.

No, it wasn't. But fairness had never been promised to them.

Katherine pulled her sister close, kissing the top of her head. "Don't worry about me," she murmured, even though terrified.

Lily didn't say anything. But she squeezed her hand as if she somehow knew.

Daniel Hahn arrived at precisely four o'clock.

Katherine sat in the parlor, her back straight as steel, her hands folded in her lap to keep them from shaking. Her mother was seated beside her, silent, as always.

Daniel entered with his father, both men carrying the same air of authority and quiet control.

He was dressed sharply in a deep navy coat and white waistcoat, his hair combed perfectly into place.

He was handsome. And he was dangerous.

Not in the way of a man who wields violence but in the way of a man who expects the world to conform to him.

Reginald extended his hand in greeting. "Daniel, welcome."

Daniel offered a polished smile, his eyes flicking briefly to Katherine. "It's always a pleasure."

Katherine's pulse pounded, but she lifted her chin and met his gaze head-on.

Daniel's smile widened slightly as if he enjoyed the challenge.

This was it. The final step is before the cage is locked

shut.

    And for the first time, Katherine realized something that sent a fresh wave of fear through her.

    She wasn't just losing her freedom.

    She was being erased.

Chapter Four: A Smile That Wasn't a Lie

The parlor at the Taylor estate was warm with the glow of afternoon light, the long shadows stretching across the fine Persian rug. The faint scent of fresh lilies and rosewater drifted through the air, mingling with the remnants of the tea served minutes ago. The fire crackled in the marble hearth, offering the space an artificial sense of comfort.

Katherine sat on the edge of a finely upholstered settee, hands folded delicately in her lap, and the smooth satin of her pale blue dress was pressed between her fingers. Across from her, Daniel Hahn and his father, Alistair Hahn, sat comfortably, their postures relaxed but poised.

Daniel's father, a broad-shouldered man with streaks of silver in his once-dark hair, held himself with effortless confidence. His gray eyes, sharp and calculating, observed Katherine with polite interest. However, they had an unmistakable weight to them—the weight of a man who saw the world in transactions and profitable alliances.

But Daniel was not his father.

Dressed in an expertly tailored navy coat, Daniel Hahn carried himself disarmingly. His chestnut hair was neatly styled, his brown eyes warm but unreadable.

When he smiled, it did not feel forced or calculated—it felt real, effortless.

And Katherine wasn't sure how she felt about that.

Her father and Alistair Hahn had been conversing for the better part of an hour, discussing business, politics, and the recent expansion of the Hahn family's shipping empire. The discussion had only briefly shifted to the real reason for this visit—their children.

"Miss Taylor, I hope you'll forgive me for speaking plainly," Alistair Hahn finally said, his voice smooth and rich, the kind of voice that had likely sealed hundreds of negotiations in his lifetime. "I've heard from many that you are quite the intelligent young woman. That is, of course, a quality my son greatly admires."

Katherine smiled, the polite, well-practiced expression she had worn a thousand times before. "You flatter me, Mr. Hahn."

Daniel's lips twitched. "He doesn't flatter, Miss Taylor. He states what is profitable."

Katherine arched a brow, her fingers tightening slightly against the fabric of her gown. "And do you speak of people as if they are profitable investments as well, Mr. Hahn?"

Daniel tilted his head, studying her for a moment. "No," he said finally. "But I do speak of circumstances as such. We all have something to gain or lose, don't we?"

Katherine's stomach clenched at the simple truth in his words. Yes, they all did.

She was supposed to dislike Daniel. That was what she had prepared for.

But he was not arrogant or dismissive. He was measured, intelligent, and even quite amusing.

And then he did something unexpected. He leaned

forward slightly, just enough that his voice lowered, just enough that only she could hear:

"I hope you won't take this the wrong way, Miss Taylor, but I have been told you are… difficult."

A tiny flicker of amusement crossed his expression.

Katherine blinked, caught between offense and intrigue. "Difficult?"

"Yes." His lips twitched. "Opinionated. Stubborn. Free-thinking."

"How utterly terrible," she murmured dryly.

Daniel let out a chuckle. "Indeed. A fate worse than death."

And before she realized it—before she even thought about it—she smiled.

A real smile.

The moment she felt it, she fought to suppress it, schooling her features back into something neutral. But it had been there. Genuine. Unbidden.

And that terrified her.

Out of the corner of her eye, she saw her father's approving glance and her mother's faint, pleased nod.

They believed the conversation had gone well.

At that moment, Katherine wasn't entirely sure they were wrong.

Later That Evening – The Streets of Boston

The cold air hit Katherine's skin like a whispered warning, but she didn't stop moving. The streets of Boston were quieter now. The sky bathed in deep hues of navy and violet, gas lamps flickering along the cobbled roads.

She should not be here.

But she had promised herself.

Finding a way out of the estate had taken careful

precision. The back gate was never left unlatched, but tonight, by sheer fortune—or perhaps fate—it had been. No doubt one of the servants had been careless or perhaps kind. Either way, she did not question it.

She hurried through the familiar streets, the sound of her soft-soled boots barely registering against the uneven pavement.

She only slowed when she saw the warm glow of light spilling from Montgomery & Son Printing Press.

And there, standing just outside the door, his sleeves rolled up to his forearms, was Elias Montgomery.

The golden glow from the shop's lanterns softened the sharp angles of his face, casting warm light over his tousled dark hair. His hazel eyes, sharp yet always filled with a quiet sort of depth, caught sight of her instantly.

Katherine barely had time to steady herself before he took a step forward.

"Katherine."

How he said her name—firm, relieved, almost disbelieving—made her chest tighten.

She did not hesitate.

She closed the distance between them and wrapped her arms around him, pressing her cheek against his shoulder. The moment he returned the embrace—his arms strong, grounding, familiar—the tension she had been carrying for days began to unravel.

For a long moment, neither of them spoke. They simply stood there, wrapped in one another's warmth, the cold Boston air forgotten.

When they finally pulled apart, Elias studied her, his expression shifting from relief to concern.

"You shouldn't be here," he murmured, though his hands lingered against her arms to confirm that she was honest and hadn't entirely disappeared into her father's world.

Katherine let out a breathless laugh that didn't quite reach her eyes. "That's becoming a common theme in my life."

Elias's brow furrowed. "Katherine."

She shook her head. "Not now. Please. Just... talk to me."

Elias exhaled slowly, his expression unreadable for a brief moment before finally gesturing toward the door. "Come inside. It's freezing out here."

The bell above the door chimed softly as she stepped into the warmth of the bookshop. The scent of ink, paper, and faint traces of coffee greeted her instantly, a comforting contrast to the suffocating floral perfumes of her home.

Elias closed the door behind them, observing her. "Does he know you're here?"

She didn't need to ask who he meant.

"My father doesn't know many things," she muttered, lightly running her fingers over a leather-bound book's spine on the nearby shelf. "And Daniel Hahn certainly doesn't."

At the mention of the name, Elias's entire demeanor changed.

His fingers curled slightly at his sides, his jaw tightening. "So it's true, then?"

Katherine hesitated. "My father wants it to be."

Elias scoffed, shaking his head. "Your father has wanted many things that you don't."

She swallowed. "This time, I don't think I'll be able to stop him."

For a moment, neither of them spoke.

The silence between them was thick with unspoken words, the result of years of knowing each other and understanding what could never be.

Elias took a slow step forward. "Katherine, you don't have to let him decide for you."

She let out a soft, bitter laugh. "And what would you have me do, Elias? Run? Where would I go? I have no money, no protection, and my father is not a man who lets go of what belongs to him."

His eyes darkened at that, at the implication of it.

"You don't belong to anyone," he said firmly.

Katherine's throat tightened, and she turned away, her hands clenching against the folds of her skirts. "It doesn't matter what I want. It never has."

Elias was silent for a long moment. Then, quietly, he said, "It matters to me."

Katherine inhaled sharply.

She had always known and felt it—the way he looked at her and his presence had always been a refuge from the life she was expected to live.

But this was the first time he had ever said it.

She turned back to him, her heart hammering. "Elias—"

Before she could say anything more, the bell above the door rang again.

Katherine's breath caught.

Elias immediately stepped forward, his presence protective as the shop door creaked open.

But it was not her father. It was not a servant sent to drag her home.

It was one of Elias's apprentices, a boy of about fifteen who worked in the printing press. He paused upon seeing them, clearly sensing the weight in the air.

"Mr. Montgomery," he said awkwardly, holding up a small package wrapped in twine. "The order for the East End is ready."

Elias exhaled, some of the tension easing from his shoulders. "Right. Set it on the desk, Henry. I'll see to it later."

The boy nodded and quickly disappeared into the back room.

Katherine turned back to Elias.

"I should go," she murmured.

He didn't argue. Maybe he knew it was useless. Maybe he knew she had already risked too much.

But as she reached for the door, his hand caught hers.

"Katherine."

She looked up at him.

His expression was different now—not just worry and frustration, but something more profound, something like certainty.

"If you ever need me," he said, quiet but firm, "you know where to find me."

Katherine felt her breath catch.

She gave him one last, lingering look—memorizing the warmth of this place, of him, of everything that had ever felt safe.

Then, without another word, she stepped out into the cold.

Chapter Five: The Night the Door Closed

The house was too quiet. Katherine had spent her entire life in the Taylor estate, enough to know its sounds —the creak of the grand staircase under the weight of morning footfalls, the faint clink of silver as the servants prepared breakfast, the hushed murmur of conversation behind closed doors. But tonight, there was nothing.

The silence stretched thick, pressing in around her like a veil.

She sat at the edge of her bed, her nightgown pooling around her ankles, her fingers gripping the folds of the fabric in her lap. The fireplace had burned low, the embers casting a faint orange glow against the far wall. The single candle on her nightstand flickered, threatening to go out, its weak flame barely illuminating the carved molding along the ceiling.

Something was wrong.

She had felt it at dinner. Her mother had been unusually quiet, and her father had barely looked at her, his presence looming over the table even as he said nothing. It was as if they were waiting for something.

Her pulse quickened as she stood, her bare feet soundless against the cold wood floor. She hesitated for only a moment before stepping toward the door, her hand reaching for the brass handle.

She needed answers.

Reginald Taylor's study smelled of leather, aged paper, and the lingering scent of pipe smoke. The fire in the hearth burned steadily, the only sound in the otherwise still room. The heavy oak desk, always a commanding presence, stood largely unburdened tonight—only a single sheet of parchment lay at its center, neatly aligned, as if it had been placed there with purpose.

Reginald sat behind it, dressed in his dark evening coat, his silver pocket watch resting beside the inkstand. He had been expecting her.

"You should be in bed, Katherine." His voice was as measured as ever, each word clipped and precise.

Katherine hesitated only a fraction before stepping fully into the room. "I need to speak with you."

He did not move. "You already have."

Her throat tightened, but she forced herself forward. "You cannot force me into this marriage," she said, steadying her voice. "I will not—"

"You misunderstand," her father interrupted, his tone mild, as if she were a child misbehaving at the dinner table. "The matter of Daniel Hahn is no longer a concern."

Confusion flickered through her, but it did not last long. Her gaze dropped to the parchment before him, to the heavy wax seal pressed into the upper corner.

The crest of Ridgefield Asylum.

Her breath hitched. The room seemed to tilt beneath her.

"What is this?" she whispered.

Reginald exhaled through his nose as if weary of her presence. "You are no longer fit to be a part of this family," he said smoothly, his fingers tapping lightly against the desk. "I will not allow your hysteria to ruin our name."

The words crashed over her, stealing the air from her lungs.

Hysteria.

The word was a sentence. A condemnation. It was the reason women disappeared behind locked doors, the reason they were stripped of their voices, their freedoms, their very existence.

She took a staggering step back. "You—you can't do this."

With deliberate slowness, Reginald reached for his quill and pressed the tip to the parchment.

He signed his name.

A sharp, helpless noise caught in her throat. Her breath came too fast, her chest rising and falling with ragged, uneven gasps. Her father had already decided.

The study suddenly felt too small, the walls too close. She turned sharply, her feet carrying her toward the door on instinct. Run. Get out. Get away.

And then she saw her.

Margaret Taylor stood in the hallway, her hazel eyes calm but unreadable, her hands folded neatly in front of her dressing gown.

Katherine stumbled to a halt, her breath still uneven.

"Mother," she choked out.

For the first time that evening, her mother's expression flickered. Just slightly. Pity, perhaps. Or regret. But whatever it was, it vanished just as quickly as it came.

"You should get some rest, dear," Margaret said softly.

It was not a suggestion.

Katherine's stomach twisted. The ground beneath her felt unsteady and unstable as if she were standing on the edge of something she could not yet see.

Her mother knew.

She had known all along.

Later the same night, the sound of footsteps in the hall woke her.

Not a servant's slow, deliberate steps nor the soft shuffle of Lily sneaking to her room in the middle of the night.

These were heavy. Unfamiliar. Purposeful.

Her eyes snapped open.

For a moment, she lay still, straining to listen. The embers in the fireplace had cooled to faint red specks, casting only the weakest glow.

Katherine barely had time to sit up before two figures entered the room. They were dressed in dark coats, their movements swift and efficient. Their faces gave away nothing.

Cold hands seized her wrists, yanking her forward. Panic flooded her system. She kicked, thrashed, fought.

"NO!" Her scream tore through the stillness, desperate, frantic. "LET ME GO!"

One of them pinned her down, their grip vice-like. A thick cloth was forced over her mouth.

The scent hit her instantly—medicinal, suffocating, overwhelming.

She writhed beneath them, her vision blurring, her mind screaming.

And then, from the corner of her vision, she saw movement in the hallway.

Her little sister stood frozen, her green eyes wide with horror.

"Katie?" she whispered.

"Lily—RUN!"

But before the little girl could move, Margaret appeared.

The last thing Katherine saw before the cloth entirely overtook her senses was Lily struggling, sobbing, and reaching for her—only to be carried away.

The world tilted violently as she was hauled outside.

The freezing air bit into her skin, but the fog in her mind kept her from fully processing it. Her body was weak, her limbs too sluggish to fight.

She was thrown into a carriage, the doors slamming shut behind her.

Her head spun. The sound of her own ragged, desperate breathing filled the space.

She turned toward the small window, her vision still blurred.

She could see the house. The estate she had known her entire life.

The front door was still open.

Her mother stood there, watching, unmoving.

And upstairs, behind the glass of a second-floor window, Lily pressed her hands against the glass, her mouth open in a silent, heartbroken sob.

The carriage lurched forward.

The wheels rattled over the cobblestone streets, carrying her away from everything she had ever known.

And then, as the night stretched long and the road turned unfamiliar, she saw it.

The iron gates of Ridgefield Asylum. The world as she had known it had ended.

Chapter Six: The First Day at Ridgefield

The first thing Katherine felt was cold. It crept through her skin, into her bones, into the very depths of her being. The cold was not simply from the temperature but from the absence of comfort, familiarity, and safety. Her mind was sluggish and disoriented, like she was trapped in the haze of a nightmare she couldn't wake from. She opened her eyes, blinking rapidly against the dim, gray light filtering into the room.

The walls were bare, a dull, lifeless gray. The bed beneath her was stiff, the mattress thin and unyielding beneath the weight of her body. A blanket, scratchy against her skin, had been draped over her. There were no embroidered pillows, no lace curtains swaying in the morning light, and no scent of roses from the garden drifting through an open window.

Nothing of home.

Katherine inhaled sharply, her hands instinctively reaching for her nightgown, only to feel coarse, unfamiliar fabric against her skin. She jerked upright.

She stared at herself in horror—her silk nightgown was gone, replaced by a plain, shapeless cotton dress, pale gray and stiff with starch. Her fingers trembled as she touched the fabric as if trying to convince herself that it wasn't real.

Her stomach lurched, her breath coming in short, uneven gasps. She wasn't home. She wasn't safe because she was in Ridgefield Asylum.

Her heart pounded as she threw back the blanket and swung her legs over the side of the bed. The floor was cold, like ice, sending a shudder through her body. She stumbled forward, her limbs weak, her movements unsteady.

The room was tiny, suffocatingly bare. A simple wooden chair sat in the corner, a metal basin rested atop a small table, and against the far wall, a narrow window with iron bars allowed the faintest sliver of daylight to filter in.

She rushed to it, her fingers curling around the bars.

Outside, the grounds of the asylum stretched before her. The morning fog clung to the earth like a ghostly veil, partially obscuring the looming iron gates in the distance. Beyond them, there was nothing but trees—dark, skeletal things that twisted toward the gray sky like outstretched hands.

A sinking dread settled in her chest.

Even if she found a way out of this room, out of this building… there was nowhere to go. Her fingers tightened around the bars until her knuckles turned white.

A sudden click from behind made her spin around and the door opened.

A woman stepped inside. She was not large or imposing, nor did she carry the same air of cold detachment that Katherine had expected. Instead, she was slender, with dark brown hair pulled into a tight bun. Her face was kind but careful, her dark eyes unreadable. She wore a simple but neat nurse's uniform—a white apron over a gray dress, sleeves rolled to her elbows, hands clasped lightly in front of her.

The woman exhaled softly. "Miss Taylor."

Katherine's throat was dry. She hadn't spoken since waking and hadn't found the strength to. She nodded.

The nurse hesitated, then stepped inside, closing the door with a quiet but unmistakable finality.

"My name is Mary-Alice," she said gently. "I am a nurse here at Ridgefield."

Katherine studied her, searching for some sign of cruelty, malice, and the cold indifference she feared would greet her here.

But she found none.

Mary-Alice moved toward the table, pouring water from a minor pitcher into a tin cup. "Drink this," she instructed, offering it to Katherine.

Katherine didn't move.

Mary-Alice sighed. "You must be thirsty. You were brought in late last night and have been asleep for hours."

Katherine's lips parted—late last night.

Memories crashed into her all at once—her bedroom door bursting open, the men restraining her, the cloth over her mouth, Lily's terrified face in the hallway, her mother's cold detachment, the carriage rattling over the cobblestone streets, the iron gates of Ridgefield slamming shut behind her.

Her breath came too fast, too shallow.

Mary-Alice must have noticed because she stepped closer, her voice gentle. "Breathe, Miss Taylor. Slowly."

Katherine forced herself to inhale, but it did little to ease the sharp panic clawing at her chest.

Mary-Alice set the cup down, observing her. "You should prepare yourself," she said after a moment. "The doctor will be coming soon."

She did not have time to process the words before the door opened again.

This time, Mary-Alice was not standing at the threshold but two attendants—large, silent men with blank expressions.

Katherine barely had time to react before they stepped forward, motioning for her to follow.

Mary-Alice did not protest. She gave Katherine a slight, unreadable nod as if silently instructing her to obey.

Katherine did not want to obey.

The corridor was long and sterile, the air thick with the scent of medicinal herbs and something faintly metallic. As she was guided through the halls, she became aware of the eyes upon her.

Some stood against the walls, their faces vacant and distant, their minds lost to whatever ghosts haunted them. Others sat on wooden benches, rocking slightly, muttering under their breath.

One woman, her gray-streaked hair hanging in tangled waves, turned her head sharply as Katherine passed.

"You shouldn't be here," she whispered.

Before she could react, one of the attendants pulled her forward.

Dr. Julian Aldridge

The office was nothing like the cold, empty room she had woken in.

It was grand and meticulously ordered. The bookshelves were lined with volumes on medicine, hysteria, and the treatment of female ailments. The scent of tobacco and ink lingered in the air, mixing with the faintest trace of something else—something sterile.

A man sat behind the desk.

Dr. Julian Aldridge.

He was younger than she had expected. His face was sharp and symmetrical, his hair neatly combed back, his piercing eyes unreadable. There was something unsettlingly precise about him, as though he existed in a world of control and calculation.

He did not speak immediately. He studied her, his gaze lingering on her features as if committing them to memory.

Katherine refused to lower her eyes.

Finally, after a long moment, he leaned back in his chair.

"You remind me of someone," he murmured.

Chapter Seven: The Doctor's Diagnosis
The Aldridge Estate

The pond behind the Aldridge house stretched out like a silver mirror beneath the midday sun, its surface shimmering, broken only by the ripples of a drifting leaf. The air smelled of fresh grass and damp earth, the scent of late summer thick in the warmth of the afternoon.

Twelve-year-old Julian Aldridge stood near the pond's edge, his shoes sinking slightly into the soft soil. His older brother, Nathaniel, stood beside him, hands shoved into his trousers pockets, eyes bright with mischief.

"You're such a girl, Julian," Nathaniel taunted, nudging him hard with his shoulder.

Julian's jaw clenched. He hated it when Nathaniel said things like that.

"I am not," he shot back, straightening his posture though his fists curled slightly at his sides.

Nathaniel smirked. "You don't even like wrestling."

Julian's face burned. He did like wrestling, but not when Nathaniel always won. His older brother was taller and stronger and always had a way of making Julian feel small, less.

Julian's irritation flared, and before he could stop

himself, he lunged at Nathaniel, shoving him backward. Nathaniel stumbled but recovered quickly, laughing.

"Oh, you have some fight in you?" Nathaniel grinned before tackling Julian to the ground.

They tumbled onto the grass, limbs entangled, grappling for control. Their struggle echoed through the open space—grunts, laughter, the sharp rustle of leaves beneath them.

From the kitchen window, Katie Aldridge watched, her hands submerged in soapy water, scrubbing dishes. Her gaze flicked up from her work, her brows knitting together as she saw her sons wrestling near the pond.

Her lips pressed into a thin line.

Julian. It was always Julian.

She turned sharply, drying her hands on a dish towel before striding toward the door.

Outside, the boys were still tangled in their fight, neither relenting.

Then, during their struggle, Julian kicked out—his foot connecting with Nathaniel's knee.

Nathaniel yelped, pulling back just as their mother's voice rang out.

"Enough!"

Katie stormed toward them, her eyes flashing with fury.

Nathaniel scrambled to his feet quickly, stepping away as Julian followed suit. His mother's sharp gaze locked onto him first.

"Julian," she hissed. "What have I told you about acting like this?"

Julian's stomach twisted. "But—"

"No." Her voice was clipped, her face taut with frustration. "I am tired of this nonsense, Julian. You always have to start trouble, don't you? Always so difficult."

Julian felt his fists clench again, but this time, it was different. It wasn't frustration at Nathaniel—it was something colder, something heavier.

Katie stepped forward. "Go inside, Nathaniel."

Nathaniel hesitated, his smirk gone, replaced with uncertainty. He glanced at Julian, then back at his mother.

"But—"

"Now."

Nathaniel gave Julian an apologetic glance before turning on his heel and jogging toward the house.

Julian stood still, his heart pounding as his mother reached for him.

Her fingers gripped his arm—too tight.

"You embarrass me," she muttered, shaking her head. "Always making a scene—"

Julian tried to step back. "I didn't—"

She yanked him closer, her breath sharp, furious.

And then—Julian stumbled with his heel caught on a patch of uneven earth. His balance shifted.

In that split second, his arm jerked against her grip, knocking her slightly off balance.

Katie staggered.

Then her face contorted into something dark, something wild.

Without thinking, without hesitation—she shoved him.

The pond's surface broke as he plunged into the water, the cold shocking the breath from his lungs. His body sank, his limbs flailing as he fought for the surface, for air, for anything to hold onto.

Above him, the light fractured into shifting golds and greens, distorted and unreachable.

Through the murky water, he saw a shadowed figure looming over him.

Julian's chest burned, his lungs tightening. His heartbeat roared in his ears. He saw a figure above him, not moving to help him. It was his mother.

Then, strong hands plunged into the water, grabbing him.

He was yanked upward, his head breaking through the surface. He gasped, sputtering, coughing, choking on air.

His father's furious voice shook the air around him.

"Katie, go inside."

Julian coughed violently, gripping his father's arms as he was dragged onto solid ground. He was shaking. His skin was cold, his breaths ragged.

Edmund's voice came again, louder, sharper.

"Inside. Now."

Katie hesitated.

Then, without a word, she turned and walked toward the house, her back rigid, unreadable.

Nathaniel stood frozen a few feet away, his face pale.

"Get up, Julian."

Julian didn't move at first, his mind still drowning in the memory of his mother's eyes and their coldness.

"Now."

Present Day – Ridgefield Asylum

Dr. Julian Aldridge sat behind his desk, his fingers lightly tapping against the polished wood. His gaze was unfocused, distant, lingering somewhere beyond the walls of Ridgefield.

Katherine observed him. Her pulse thundered in her

ears, her hands clenched tightly in her lap. She had been so sure he was about to speak, but instead, he sat there, lost in his thoughts.

Then, suddenly, his gaze snapped back to her. Katherine flinched though she tried to suppress it. Dr. Aldridge blinked as if shaking off whatever had gripped him. His fingers stopped their rhythmic tapping.

He reached for the notebook beside him, rapidly flipping it open.

"You do not behave like most women brought here," he said finally, his voice smooth, detached, but now laced with something else.

Katherine swallowed hard, but she did not let her voice waver.

"And how do most women behave?"

Dr. Aldridge didn't answer immediately. He studied her, his gaze lingering, calculating.

Then, in a tone too casual, too deliberate, he said: "You remind me of someone."

Katherine felt a chill skitter down her spine. She did not know who he meant.

But for the first time since arriving at Ridgefield, she realized something far more terrifying than the asylum itself.

She had caught the attention of a man who should terrify her.

And she did not know why.

Chapter Eight: The Weight of Betrayal

The Taylor Estate

The study was silent except for the faint scratching of a quill against parchment. Reginald Taylor sat behind his massive mahogany desk, the flickering candlelight casting long shadows across the walls of his private office. Stacks of ledgers and legal documents lay in perfect order, untouched, except for the one he was signing now.

There was no sign that a daughter had been taken from this house just nights ago. No remnants of grief, no indication of loss.

The heavy door creaked open, and Margaret Taylor stepped inside, her hands clasped tightly at her waist. She hesitated before speaking, her voice softer than usual, as if she already knew what kind of response awaited her.

"Have you checked on Katherine?"

Reginald did not pause in his writing or even lift his eyes. "Why should I?"

Margaret flinched. "She is our daughter, Reginald."

He dipped the quill again, signing his name with an unshaken hand. "Not anymore."

The words punched the breath from her lungs. She swallowed hard, stepping closer, though her fingers trembled at her sides.

"She is still alive," Margaret pressed. "She is still

ours."

Reginald finally looked up, his cold hazel eyes locking onto hers. "She is gone, Margaret. She is where she belongs."

Margaret's vision blurred with tears. "And where is that? A place where they will silence her, break her? Do you even care what happens to her?"

Reginald leaned back in his chair, exuding the same unwavering composure that had once made her feel safe. Now, it only terrified her.

"You will not speak of her again," he said as if the matter were settled as if Katherine had never existed.

Margaret let out a ragged breath. "She will never forgive us."

Reginald's expression did not change. "She has no choice."

A choked sob left her lips, and before she could stop herself, she turned sharply, rushing from the room. The heavy wooden door slammed behind her, echoing through the house like a final verdict.

In the hallway, Martha stood frozen, her breath caught in her throat. She had not meant to overhear. She had only been dusting the sitting room when she heard the sharp voices, the tension crackling through the air. Something had told her to pause, to listen. And now— now she wished she hadn't.

Katherine was gone—not married, not traveling, gone. With shaking hands, she backed away, slipping into the small linen room down the corridor. She closed the door softly behind her, pressing a hand against her mouth. Tears burned behind her eyes as she struggled to make sense of it. She had raised Katherine and watched her grow from a bright-eyed little girl into a strong-willed young woman. She had dressed her for balls, comforted her on nights when she couldn't sleep and brushed out her golden hair while listening to her dreams.

And now she was gone—because of them. A single tear slid down Martha's cheek as she leaned against the shelves, trying to understand how a father could do such a thing.

Margaret walked outside, the cool evening air wrapping around her like a thin shroud. The garden was still, the roses along the pathway wilting slightly under the weight of the season. She inhaled deeply as if breathing the night air could erase the weight in her chest. She had agreed to let them take her.

Her hands trembled as she reached out, brushing the delicate petals of a white rose. Katherine had always loved white roses. As a child, she picked them, pressing them into books and tucking them into her hair. Would her daughter ever walk in these gardens again? Would she ever forgive her? A cool breeze stirred the air, rustling the hedges around her, but it did nothing to still the ache inside her.

Upstairs, Lily lay curled in her bed, silent tears slipping down her cheeks. Her arms wrapped around the stuffed rabbit Katherine had given her on her fifth birthday, the worn fabric damp where she clutched it against her chest. She had barely spoken since that night. The night she had seen Katherine dragged away.

She squeezed her eyes shut, but the images would not leave her—the men, the way they had grabbed her sister, the way Katherine had screamed for her to run. The way Mother had pulled her away, whispering that it was for the best. It wasn't for the best. A small sob broke from her lips, and she pressed her face deeper into her pillow. But somehow, she knew that was impossible.

The Hahn Estate

Daniel Hahn paced his father's study, his hands clenched behind his back. His father, Alistair Hahn, sat behind his desk, arms crossed over his chest.

"I don't understand," Daniel said tightly. "Why was the engagement called off?"

His father barely glanced up. "Because she is unwell."

Daniel's frown deepened. "Katherine is not unwell."

Alistair exhaled, sifting through the papers. "Her father has deemed her so. And if he has, then it is out of your hands."

"That's not good enough."

Alistair finally set down his pen, looking at his son thoroughly. "You should be relieved, Daniel. You would not have had a wife. You would have had a burden."

Daniel's jaw locked.

"She was never a burden," he said, his voice sharp.

Alistair sighed, leaning back in his chair. "If you care for her at all, you will move on. She is no longer your concern."

But Daniel wasn't listening anymore. A sick feeling twisted in his stomach. Something was wrong, and he intended to find out what.

Taylor Estate

Daniel stood in Reginald Taylor's office, his fists clenched.

"Where is she?"

Reginald barely looked up from his documents. "That is no longer your concern."

Daniel's pulse thundered. "She was supposed to be my wife. That makes it my concern."

Reginald exhaled sharply, setting his quill aside. His expression remained unreadable, but there was something cold beneath it.

"You would do well to forget her," Reginald said flatly. "She is where she belongs."

Daniel's stomach twisted. That was not an answer; it was a dismissal and made him more determined.

Ridgefield Asylum

Mary-Alice combed through Katherine's tangled hair, working slowly and carefully. The young woman sat motionless, her eyes distant, staring at nothing.

Her hands rested limply in her lap, and her lips parted slightly as if she had forgotten how to close them.

Mary-Alice sighed. She had seen this before. The effects of medication. The haze of compliance. She dipped a cloth into warm water and gently wiped the corner of Katherine's mouth.

Katherine blinked as if stirring from a fog. Then, without warning, a single tear slipped down her cheek.

Mary-Alice swallowed hard, placing the comb aside. She reached out, hesitating—then gently, lightly, placed a hand over Katherine's trembling fingers. And for the first time, Mary-Alice wondered if she was watching someone slowly lose themselves.

Chapter Nine: A Prison of Their Making

Katherine had lost all sense of time. The days in Ridgefield bled together, each moment stretching into the next with no relief. There were no clocks in her room, no indicators of morning or night. She only knew the time had passed when food was placed before her—bland porridge, hardened bread, weak tea that tasted of nothing. She barely touched it. Sleep eluded her, haunted by the sounds of distant wailing, the shuffle of feet beyond the door, and the occasional clang of metal against stone.

When the door swung open, she flinched.

A broad-shouldered man stepped inside, his presence filling the space. He had the build of a laborer, muscular with thick arms that strained against his gray uniform. A deep scar ran across his right cheekbone, disappearing into the bristle of his beard. He was not a doctor or a nurse—an orderly.

"On your feet," he ordered, his voice flat, uninterested.

Katherine remained seated, gripping the rough fabric of her dress. "Where are you taking me?"

He exhaled through his nose, unimpressed with her defiance. "Dr. Aldridge wants to see you."

A deep unease settled in her stomach.

Her silence must have been enough because he stepped forward, reaching for her arm. She recoiled when his fingers grazed her sleeve, twisting away from his grip.

"No. I won't go."

He let out a weary sigh as though he had expected as much. He reached for her again, but she fought back. Katherine thrashed, shoved at his chest, and kicked against his shin, her fear outweighing her exhaustion. He stumbled slightly but recovered, his grip tightening as she flailed in his hold.

"Enough," he growled, but she only struggled harder.

Her voice rang out, raw and desperate. "Let me go! I don't belong here! You have no right!"

A shadow moved in the doorway. Another figure entered—a tall, severe-looking nurse in a pristine uniform. Her auburn hair was braided tightly against her scalp, her features sharp and void of sympathy. Without a word, she reached into her apron pocket and withdrew a small glass vial and syringe.

Katherine froze, her breath coming in sharp gasps.

"Hold her still," the nurse instructed.

She twisted in the orderly's grip, panic clawing at her throat. "No, please—"

The needle pierced her arm before she could finish. A burn spread through her veins, creeping into her limbs and dulling her movements. Her body sagged, her mind turning thick and sluggish. The fight drained from her as darkness pulled her under.

The last thing she saw was Mary-Alice standing in the hallway, her eyes wide with horror.

The moment Katherine regained consciousness, she knew something was wrong.

She was cold. Unbearably, agonizingly cold.

Her body felt heavy and constricted. Her arms and legs were pressed against her sides, wrapped tightly in something damp and suffocating. The weight of it crushed her ribs, making every breath a battle.

The air smelled of mildew, the walls damp with lingering moisture. Shadows flickered in the dim room, their movements distorted by the haze in her mind.

"She's awake."

A voice, distant and detached.

She tried to move, but her body refused. The wet sheets clung to her like a second skin, soaked in ice-cold water, their purpose clear—to weaken, exhaust, and strip her of resistance.

"Please," her voice cracked, barely more than a whisper.

A figure stood at the edge of the room—another nurse, older and plump, her features lined with indifference. She checked a small clock on the wall and then looked at Katherine.

"You'll be unwrapped when the doctor sees fit," she said without emotion. "That may be in an hour. Or four."

The words crashed over her like a wave.

Tears burned behind her eyes, but she refused to cry, refused to let them see her break. How could her parents do this? How had her father quickly signed his name, condemning her to this place?

No one would come for her. No one would hear her.

Across the city, Elias Montgomery turned the page of the ledger before him but could not remember a single number he had written.

He sat behind the wooden counter of his family's bookshop, his fingers idly tracing the spine of a leather-bound novel. He was supposed to be focused—new shipments needed to be cataloged, orders placed, and shelves arranged. But his mind had been elsewhere for days.

Katherine.

He had tried not to think of her and accepted that she was meant to marry another. But the thoughts still came, creeping in during the quiet moments, haunting him like an unfinished story.

He remembered how her eyes lit up when she spoke of the future. The way her laugh had softened even his worst days.

A voice called his name, snapping him from his thoughts. A teenage apprentice stood in the doorway, waiting for instruction. Elias pushed the thoughts aside, forcing himself to focus.

Even as he did, her ghost lingered.

Margaret adjusted the hood of her cloak, glancing over her shoulder before stepping toward Ridgefield's iron gates.

Her pulse pounded. She knew she should not be here.

The asylum loomed before her, its high stone walls casting long shadows in the evening light.

A guard intercepted her before she could take another step.

"Mrs. Taylor," he greeted, his tone cool but firm.

She hesitated, her voice unsteady. "I am here to see my daughter."

The man did not move. "That is not permitted."

Margaret stiffened. "I have the right—"

"You signed the papers," he interrupted. "You agreed to the rules. If you attempt to see her again, you will violate them."

The words stole her breath.

The reality of it all crashed over her like a wave—Katherine was no longer hers to see.

Tears stung her eyes as she turned away, her steps slow, her heart splintering with everyone.

Daniel stood in Reginald Taylor's office. His hands balled into fists.

"You sent her to Ridgefield."

Reginald did not look up. "She is unwell."

Daniel's breath came hard and fast, his anger barely contained. "She is not unwell. You did this to control her."

Reginald exhaled, finally setting down his pen. "You should be relieved, Daniel. You would have married a burden."

Daniel's chest tightened with rage. "I will not stand for this. You will not get away with it."

Reginald met his gaze, calm and unaffected. "And what do you intend to do?"

Daniel didn't have an answer. Not yet. But he swore to himself—he would not let Katherine rot in that place.

No matter the cost.

Chapter Eleven: Shattered Composure

The Taylor estate was quiet, but there was no peace within its walls. The tension hummed through the halls, thick as a storm about to break. Daniel Hahn strode through the grand entryway, his footsteps sharp and unyielding against the polished floor. He was done with waiting, done with silence. This time, he was going to get answers. Servants shrank away as he passed, their gazes flickering toward the closed doors of Reginald Taylor's office. They knew better than to interfere. Daniel pushed the doors open without knocking.

Reginald sat at his desk, his brown eyes lifting only slightly, filled with irritation rather than surprise. The papers before him remained untouched, but the candlelight flickered, casting long shadows over his face.

"You again," Reginald muttered, setting his quill aside. "What now, Daniel?"

Daniel stepped forward, his jaw tight, voice seething. "I know for certain now. You sent Katherine to Ridgefield."

Reginald exhaled sharply. "I already told you—"

"You told me she was sick. That she needed help," Daniel snapped. "But you never said where. You never admitted what you did. You locked her away in that place — "that prison"—and now you expect the world to move on?"

Reginald's expression did not change. "Because it already has."

Daniel slammed his fist against the desk, making the papers flutter. "Not for me. Not for the people who care about her."

Reginald's lips curled into something resembling amusement. "You seem quite invested for a man who no longer has a claim to her."

"Because she was stolen from her life!" Daniel shot back. "From me. From Lily. From everyone who loved her."

Reginald sighed, his patience wearing thin. "Katherine was out of control. She had no sense of duty. She has no regard for her family's reputation. She made her choice, and I made mine."

Daniel's hands curled into fists at his sides. "She was seventeen, Reginald. A girl. She was supposed to have choices."

Reginald's calm mask cracked—just slightly.

"Enough," he said coldly. "You are young, Daniel. You do not understand the burdens that come with power."

Daniel's breath was ragged with fury. "If being a man of power means sacrificing your daughter, then I never want to understand it."

Reginald's expression darkened. "Leave. And do not return unless you are willing to act like a man and let this go."

Daniel leaned forward, his voice low and firm.

"I will never let this go."

Then he turned, storming out of the office.

Martha sat on the edge of Lily's bed, smoothing out

the creases in the quilt with careful, deliberate hands.

Lily sat cross-legged, her blue eyes round and full of questions.

"Martha," she murmured, clutching her stuffed rabbit tightly. "Father says Katie is sick."

Martha's fingers stilled.

Lily continued her voice barely above a whisper. "Is she?"

Martha swallowed against the tightness in her throat. What could she say? How could she lie when she had seen the truth with her own eyes?

Lily's lower lip trembled. "She would have written to me."

Martha looked away. "Maybe she cannot."

Lily's brows furrowed. "Why not?"

Martha hesitated. "Sometimes, when people are unwell, they need rest."

Lily tilted her head. "But if she's resting, why can't I see her?"

Martha's breath caught. Lily was smart. Too smart. And deep down, she already knew the answer.

The carriage rocked violently as Margaret Taylor leaned forward, gripping the edge of the seat. She could see Ridgefield's tall iron gates, their cold, unforgiving presence looming against the gray sky. The moment the carriage stopped, she flung open the door and stepped onto the damp earth.

The guards were already watching her. She ignored them. She needed to see her daughter.

"Katherine Taylor," she announced breathlessly. "I demand to see her."

The guards did not move.

"Mrs. Taylor," one of them finally said, his voice

carefully measured. "You are not permitted inside."

Margaret's chest tightened. "She is my daughter!"

"You signed her over to Dr. Aldridge," the man reminded her indifferently.

Margaret's vision blurred. Tears burned behind her eyes. "That was a mistake," she whispered.

"It is done."

Margaret rushed toward the gate, hands clutching the bars.

"Katherine!" she screamed.

The wind howled in response.

"Katherine, I'm here!"

The guards grabbed her by the arms, pulling her back. She fought against them, kicking, sobbing, screaming.

"I need to see her!" she begged. "Please, she's just a girl—she needs me!"

The guards forced her back toward the carriage.

She thrashed in their grip. "You cannot keep a mother from her child!"

But the answer was already evident as they shoved her inside and closed the door. They could and they had.

Elias had spent weeks convincing himself that Katherine had left by choice. That she had married another. That she had moved on. But when he heard the name Ridgefield, something inside him shattered. He had been stocking shelves in the family bookshop when he overheard the two women whispering near the front counter.

"… Ridgefield is where families send their daughters when they have nowhere else to go."

His blood ran cold.

Another voice.

"They say it's a place for the insane, but truly… it is a place for those who refuse to conform."

Elias froze.

Ridgefield. His heart slammed against his ribs. Had Katherine been sent there? The thought clawed at his mind, refusing to let go. He had been so sure she had left willingly, but now… now there was doubt. Terrifying, undeniable doubt. And Elias was going to find the truth no matter what it took.

Chapter Twelve: Fractured Bonds

The cold had settled deep into Katherine's bones. Two days had passed since she had been released from Seclusion, but she felt no freer than she had behind that locked door. Ridgefield itself was a prison, and every room, every corridor, every breath she took within its walls was suffocating. She ached from head to toe, her body still weak from hunger and exhaustion. Her lips were cracked, her throat dry, and the meager portions of food given to her barely kept the dizziness at bay.

Mary-Alice did what she could. She smuggled extra scraps of bread, sat beside Katherine when others ignored her and spoke softly in ways that reminded her of what it was like to be human. But even she was beginning to lose her grip on Katherine's slipping mind.

"Katherine," Mary-Alice whispered as she tucked a thin woolen blanket around her trembling shoulders. "You mustn't give up."

Katherine didn't respond. She barely felt the weight of the blanket against her skin. She had stopped fighting because what was the point? She had been moved out of Seclusion a day ago and placed among the other patients. But that had not been a mercy—it had been another form of torment. The women around her were not dangerous, but their strange, vacant stares unsettled her. Some whispered to people who were not there, others rocked back and forth in a quiet, endless rhythm.

One woman wept softly in the corner, clutching a torn scrap of lace, muttering, "Mama's coming. Mama's coming."

Another sat perfectly still, staring straight ahead, blinking so infrequently that Katherine wondered if she was breathing.

Her stomach twisted. This would be her fate if she stayed. Would she become like them? Forgotten? Left to rot in a place where no one cared if she lived or died? She closed her eyes, desperate to escape the moment, and suddenly, she was somewhere else—somewhere warm.

Katherine remembers a moment with her mother. Her mother sat beside her in the chaise lounge in the sitting room, hands folded neatly over her lap. Lily was curled against Katherine's side, her golden curls tickling Katherine's chin as she hummed softly to herself. Her father was not with them. He never was. Reginald Taylor preferred the solitude of his study, where business occupied him far more than his wife and daughters ever did.

Katherine had been grateful for his absence. His quick temper and sharp voice had always made her stomach twist with unease, but Lily had suffered the most from his moods. She remembered when Lily was only six years old, too young to fully understand rules and mistakes.

Reginald had been in a foul mood that day, his patience threadbare, his voice a storm brewing with each reprimand. Lily had spilled ink onto his desk, and before anyone could stop it, his hand had raised—fast, sharp, merciless. Lily had shrunk back, eyes wide with terror. Katherine had stepped between them without thinking, without hesitation.

"She's just a child!" she had screamed.

Reginald's fury had been swift, but not for Lily. Katherine had borne the punishment instead. Their mother had said nothing—not then, not ever. She had merely pressed a shaking hand against her lips, her eyes glassy and distant. Katherine had wanted to hate her for her silence, but even as a child, she had known the truth. Her mother had been just as much a prisoner as they were.

A sudden shift brought Katherine back to the present. Someone had sat beside her. Katherine blinked, slowly turning her head toward the woman who occupied the chair beside her. She was about twenty-five years old, her dark brown hair matted and tangled, and her eyes a shade of green that once might have been bright. But now, they were dulled and unfocused.

"Five years," the woman murmured.

Katherine frowned. "What?"

The woman tilted her head, her lips twitching into something that was not quite a smile. "Or six. I don't know anymore."

Katherine's stomach tightened. "You've been here that long?"

The woman turned to her fully now, her green eyes locking onto Katherine's in an eerie, unwavering stare.

"I stopped counting after the first year," she whispered. "It's easier that way."

Katherine's breath came sharp. Was this her future? A life of blurred years and forgotten time? She had to get out.

Daniel stood before his father, rage burning in his chest. Alistair Hahn studied him from across the sitting room, his expression of calm disapproval.

"Katherine is at Ridgefield," Daniel said, his voice shaking with barely contained fury. "Something terrible has happened to her. I need to get her out."

Alistair sighed, setting his brandy glass aside. "Daniel, if Katherine is sick, you don't need a wife like that."

Daniel's hands curled into fists.

Alistair continued, his voice maddeningly calm. "You need a good, respectable wife of social standing. Someone who will obey you, honor you and perform her duties properly. Not a broken girl in an asylum."

Disgust curdled in Daniel's stomach.

"You sound just like Reginald."

Alistair's eyes flickered with warning. "Mind your tongue."

Daniel took a step forward. "I will not leave her in that place. Katherine will be my wife, and I will bring her home."

Alistair sighed, shaking his head. "You are making a mistake."

Daniel's voice was steel. "No. The mistake was letting her suffer this long."

Martha and Lily are quiet in the dining room. Martha placed a small plate of fruit and vegetables in front of Lily, sitting across from her in the quiet afternoon light. The girl's small fingers toyed with a strawberry, her blue eyes filled with uncertainty and sadness.

"Katie is coming home," Lily whispered.

Martha hesitated. "I hope so, sweetheart."

Lily's eyes shone with determination.

"No. I know it."

Martha's heart broke for small, sweet Lily, who

didn't understand the cruelty of this life.

Margaret stood before her husband, her hands clenched at her sides, her heart hammering. Reginald looked up from his papers, unimpressed by her presence.

"I never wanted to marry you," she said, her voice more substantial than expected.

Reginald's brow lifted.

"You disgust me," she continued. "I only married you because I had to."

Reginald's expression darkened. The slap came fast, sharp, a crack of skin against skin. Margaret gasped, her head snapping to the side.

"You will obey me," Reginald said coldly. "You will stop defying me. You know your place."

Margaret lifted her chin, ignoring the sting on her cheek. Her place had once been behind him. But not anymore. She now knows that her place is now behind her husband.

Chapter Thirteen: Unraveling Truths

The cold air bit Elias's skin as he rode through the city streets, the weight of unease pressing heavily against his chest. He had spent too many nights lying awake, consumed by the gnawing feeling that something was wrong. That Katherine hadn't left him—she had been taken. And now, there was no room left for doubt. He had to find Daniel Hahn.

When the Hahn estate came into view, its grand columns standing proudly against the darkened sky, Elias felt the full force of his exhaustion settled over him. His limbs ached, his body heavy, and his fever worsened. But there was no time to be weak. A servant opened the door, but before Elias could speak, Alistair Hahn appeared.

The older man's eyes narrowed in disdain. "Montgomery."

Elias lifted his chin. "I need to see Daniel."

Alistair scoffed, blocking the doorway. "Whatever business you have with my son, it ends here. Get off my property."

Elias's chest burned with frustration. "This is about Katherine Taylor."

Alistair's mouth curled into a sneer. "Katherine Taylor is no longer a concern to this family."

Elias took a step forward, his stance unwavering.

"She is to me."

The tension thickened between them, but Elias refused to back down.

"If you don't leave," Alistair warned, "I will remove you."

Before Elias could respond, a voice cut through the air.

"Let him in."

Alistair turned sharply, his expression darkening as Daniel stepped into the entryway.

Daniel's eyes met Elias's, filled with something between suspicion and urgency. "If this is about Katherine, I want to hear it."

Alistair's jaw clenched, but he stepped aside. Daniel led Elias into the study, closing the doors behind them.

"What do you know?" Daniel demanded.

Elias's breathing was uneven, his hands trembling slightly. "I know she didn't leave by choice. I heard whispers about Ridgefield... and now know she's there."

Daniel's expression hardened. "She is."

Elias ran a hand over his face. "God…"

Daniel observed him, his eyes narrowing.

Elias waved him off. "We need to get Katherine out."

Daniel hesitated only a moment before speaking. "Will you help me?"

Elias met his gaze without hesitation. "I would die before I let her stay in that place."

The night air was cool as Lily sat by the window, hugging her knees to her chest. The moonlight cast silver shadows across the floor, but the warmth Katherine had always brought into the house was missing. Tears slid silently down her cheeks.

"Katie," she whispered into the night.

The sound of quiet sobbing echoed from the hallway.

Margaret Taylor stood just outside Lily's door, her hands covering her mouth, her body trembling. She had failed her daughter—both of them. Swallowing back her tears, Margaret composed herself and stepped inside. Lily wiped her eyes quickly, trying to hide her sorrow. Margaret sat beside her, gently stroking her golden curls.

"Would you like to hear a story?" she whispered.

Lily sniffled but nodded.

Margaret closed her eyes for a moment before beginning.

"Once, in a land where the sun always kissed the earth, there was a beautiful bird with golden feathers. She was the brightest creature in the forest, and all who saw her admired her beauty. But what made her truly special was her song. It was sweeter than honey, stronger than any wind, and even the saddest hearts would smile when she sang."

Lily blinked up at her mother, captivated.

Margaret continued, her voice soft. "But one day, a cruel man took the bird and locked her away, saying that her song was too wild, too free. He built a cage of gold and told her she must never sing again."

Lily's small hands clutched the fabric of her nightdress.

Margaret swallowed. "But the bird knew that even the strongest cage could not keep her voice silent forever. And so, she waited and sang—not for the cruel man, but for those who still listened. And one day, the wind carried her song far beyond the bars of her prison. Someone heard her."

Lily's breath hitched. "And what happened?"

Margaret kissed the top of her head. "They set her free."

Lily curled against her mother's side for the first time in weeks and fell asleep peacefully. Margaret stared at the ceiling, blinking back fresh tears. Katherine, hold on.

In the dimly lit servants' quarters, Martha wrung her hands. Across from her, another maid—Eliza Harper, a petite woman with dark brown hair tucked beneath a cap—watched her with concern.

"She's alive," Martha whispered, her voice thick with emotion. "Katherine is alive at Ridgefield."

Eliza's eyes widened. "You're sure?"

Martha nodded. "I heard Mr. Hahn and Daniel arguing about it."

Eliza's hands clenched into fists. "That poor girl..."

"We have to do something," Martha whispered. "If we don't... I fear she'll never return."

Eliza exhaled shakily. "What can we do?"

Martha's expression hardened.

"We find a way to get her out."

Katherine sat in the dim corner of the common room, her mind still trapped between the past and present. The woman beside her—the same eerie patient from before—stared at her with unblinking green eyes. Katherine turned slightly, hesitant.

"Why are you here?" she finally asked.

The woman's lips twitched. "Why are you?"

Katherine didn't answer.

The woman leaned forward slightly, her voice a whisper barely above the fireplace crackle.

"I had a father like yours once. He decided I was troublesome. That I was better... forgotten."

Katherine's stomach tightened.

The woman's fingers traced the hem of her sleeve. "I had a fiancé—a kind man. But my father had other plans. He sent me here."

Katherine felt the world tilt beneath her. Would that be her fate? Would she lose track of the years, the seasons, and herself?

"I should have fought harder," the woman murmured. "But I didn't. And now, I am a ghost."

Katherine's breath shook. She had to escape. Before, she, too, was forgotten.

Chapter Fourteen: Fractured Realities

Was the stew gray, or was it brown? Katherine wasn't sure anymore. It smelled of nothing, tasted of nothing, just a thick, lukewarm sludge that turned her stomach. She stirred it absently, watching how it clung to the wooden spoon, unwilling to slip away—a grotesque metaphor for Ridgefield itself.

"Don't think about it too much," a voice murmured beside her.

Katherine lifted her head and stared into a pair of piercing green eyes.

Eleanor Whitmore.

As she introduced herself, Ellie had dark brown hair that once might have been soft but now hung in tangled waves. She was pale, her frame slender, as if Ridgefield had been slowly consuming her. But her eyes were still alive.

"You'll make yourself sick if you think too much about what's in it," Ellie said, stirring her bowl without lifting her spoon.

Katherine hesitated. "I'm not sure I care anymore."

Ellie smirked, though it lacked warmth. "You will. Give it time."

A pause.

"Did your father send you here?" Ellie asked,

observing Katherine.

Katherine stiffened, her grip tightening around the spoon.

"Yes."

Ellie exhaled sharply. "Mine too. Fathers always know best, don't they?"

Katherine didn't respond, but she felt the weight of those words settle in her chest.

Ellie leaned forward slightly. "You still believe someone is coming for you, right?"

Katherine swallowed. "Someone will come."

Ellie stared at her for a long moment before giving her a small, sad smile.

"I hope you're right."

The Cobblestone streets of Boston were still bustling, filled with the clatter of carriage wheels and murmuring voices. Lily clutched her coat tighter around herself, her little boots clicking hurriedly against the pavement. People stared. Some whispered, some pointed. But no one stopped her. No one helped. Her breaths came in frantic puffs of white as she turned a corner, her heart pounding. She had to find Katie. A shadow loomed over her, and a voice—firm but kind—spoke.

"Little one."

Lily froze.

A man knelt before her, his dark brows furrowed in concern. His uniform told her he was necessary—a police officer.

"What's your name?" he asked gently.

Lily lifted her chin. "I'm Lily."

The officer's features softened. "Lily, do you know where your home is?"

She nodded, but her tiny hands curled into fists. "I'm

not going home. I have to find Katie."

The officer hesitated. "Who is Katie?"

"My sister," Lily whispered.

His brows knitted together. "Where is she?"

Lily bit her lip. "She's resting. But she needs me."

The officer exhaled. He had seen lost children before. Grieving, confused, searching for someone they would never find.

"Lily, what are your parents' names?"

She huffed. "Mom and Dad."

A small smile flickered on his lips. "And what do other people call them?"

Lily thought for a moment. "Mr. and Mrs. Taylor."

The officer's expression changed. Reginald Taylor. He knew that name. A man of power, a man of cruelty. And now his daughter was wandering the streets alone? Something was wrong.

"Lily, I have to take you home."

"No!" she screamed and bolted.

"Lily, wait!"

Officer Robert Michaels lunged for her, but the child was quick. By the time he pushed through the crowd, she was gone.

Dr. Aldridge remembered his youth as he did often. The room was dark, except for the soft glow of candlelight flickering against the walls. The house had been silent for hours, but Julian Aldridge lay awake, small and trembling beneath his blankets. Footsteps echoed in the hall. He squeezed his eyes shut. If he pretended to be asleep, maybe she wouldn't— The door creaked open. His heart pounded. A woman's silhouette appeared in the doorway.

Katie Aldridge.

"Julian," she whispered.

He didn't move.

"Julian," she repeated, sharper this time.

He opened his eyes, his throat tight.

His mother stood over him, her nightgown flowing like a ghost's veil, her eyes deep, dark pits of something unreadable.

"You were bad today," she murmured.

Julian's hands curled into the sheets.

"I—I tried to be good."

His mother's lips pressed together. "You didn't try hard enough."

Julian's stomach twisted.

This was how it always began.

"You are my greatest sin," she whispered, brushing a hand through his hair like one would comfort a child before delivering the punishment.

Julian forced himself not to flinch.

"If I am bad," he whispered, "how do I become good?"

His mother's nails scraped against his scalp.

"You don't."

Katherine shivered as she was led into Dr. Aldridge's office. The moment she entered, he was already staring at her. Not at her, but through her.

"Katie," he murmured.

Katherine's breath hitched. He wasn't looking at her. He was looking through her.

"Miss Katie," he whispered.

Katherine's pulse thundered. "Who is Katie?"

Dr. Aldridge's jaw clenched, his fingers tightening against the desk.

"She was there," he muttered, "when I was a boy."

His eyes were vacant, lost in some twisted memory. Katherine's throat tightened.

His fingers twitched against the desk. "She used to bring me broth when I misbehaved."

Katherine felt sick.

Dr. Aldridge's voice dropped. "I tried to be good. But I could never be good." A flicker of something terrifying passed over his face.

"You remind me of her."

Katherine stiffened. "I want to see Lily."

Dr. Aldridge's eyes sharpened. "There is no Lily."

The world shattered. Katherine's lungs seized. No Lily. Her hands clutched the arms of the chair, her body trembling.

"Where is she?" she whispered.

Dr. Aldridge tilted his head. "She never existed."

A broken sob escaped Katherine's lips. She couldn't breathe. Lily was gone. She was dead.

The scream ripped from her throat. Hands grabbed the sharp jab of a needle.

She fought, screamed, thrashed—until her limbs turned to lead.

Cold air. Water. The ice consumed her, then— silence.

Chapter Fifteen: A Mind Unraveling

The walls pressed in. They had always been close, suffocating, but now they seemed to breathe, shifting inward, swallowing the last remnants of space. The room was damp and frigid, the smell of mildew clinging to every corner.

Katherine sat curled against the rough cot, her arms wrapped tightly around her knees. Her gown clung to her damp skin, still carrying the icy remnants of the water they had plunged her into. The memory sent a shudder down her spine, but she barely noticed.

Her mind drifted, stretched too thin, unraveling thread by thread.

Lily.

The thought struck like a dagger to her chest.

She squeezed her eyes shut, willing herself to hear the soft hum of her little sister's voice. The warmth of her laughter. She would curl into Katherine's lap, wrapping tiny arms around her waist as if she could hold the whole world together with her embrace.

But it was gone. Instead, a voice—small, delicate—whispered through the darkness.

Katie... Katie... where are you?

Katherine's breath hitched. Her head snapped up, her pulse hammering.

"Lily?" she rasped, her throat raw, barely able to form the word.

No response.

Just silence.

Then—a giggle, high and soft, like a child playing a cruel game of hide-and-seek. Katherine twisted toward the door, her heart slamming against her ribs.

"Lily?" Her voice cracked, desperate.

She clenched her fists, her nails digging into her palms until pain cut through the haze in her mind. Lily had been real. Hadn't she? Her father always told her she was prone to dramatic fits, that she imagined things, and that her mind wandered too far beyond reason. Had Lily ever existed at all? Or had she been nothing more than a dream? A sob clawed at Katherine's throat. She didn't know what was real anymore. And that terrified her more than anything.

Outside the door, Mary-Alice hesitated. She could hear Katherine murmuring, her voice a frayed whisper —a girl unraveling, inch by inch. Mary-Alice's fingers trembled against the keys at her waist. She could sit by her, offer quiet comfort, and tell her she wasn't alone. But the walls had ears and kindness could be dangerous. Instead, she forced herself to move down the hall, her footsteps swallowed by the heavy silence of Ridgefield. Ahead, two nurses whispered in hushed tones, their voices carrying through the dimly lit corridor.

"She reminds him of her."

Mary-Alice slowed her steps.

"The new patient?"

A nod. "She looks like his mother, doesn't she?"

A chill slithered down Mary-Alice's spine.

The second nurse shuddered. "It's unnatural, the

way he watches her."

Mary-Alice felt her breath shorten. She turned swiftly, her feet carrying her down the hall until she reached the record room. Her fingers trembled as she rifled through the files, flipping through pages worn with time. Then—she found it. Katherine Ann Taylor. Her name stood out in crisp, inked script, elegant and damning. The patient notes were routine at first—admittance date, symptoms of "hysteria." But at the bottom of the file, written in Aldridge's neat, precise handwriting, were three chilling words:

"Observation indefinitely. No release."

Mary-Alice's stomach dropped. Katherine was never meant to leave Ridgefield.

Daniel is meeting Elias. Daniel's fists curled tightly as he paced Elias's small room.

"She isn't coming out of there." His voice was clipped, strained. "Not unless we force her out."

Elias sat hunched on the edge of the bed, his complexion pale, beads of sweat clinging to his brow. He was thinner than he had been just weeks ago, the sickness wearing him down. But his eyes remained sharp.

"You're going back?" Elias asked, observing Daniel.

Daniel turned, his expression unreadable. "I have no choice."

Elias exhaled, his breath ragged. "You'll get yourself killed."

Daniel's jaw clenched. "If you have a better plan, I'd love to hear it."

Silence stretched between them, thick with unspoken fears. Elias shifted, his hands tightening in his lap.

"We need leverage," he said finally. "Someone inside.

Someone willing to betray Ridgefield."

Daniel hesitated. "That could take weeks."

Elias's breath came out slow. "Or it could take one well-placed bribe."

There is a tense pause. Then, Daniel exhaled sharply, rubbing a hand over his face.

"Fine," he muttered. "Then we find someone willing to talk."

Because if they didn't act soon, there wouldn't be anything left of Katherine to save.

The servant's quarters were dark, the flickering candlelight casting uneasy shadows against the stone walls. Martha's hands shook as she turned the page in the record book, her breath quickening.

"Eliza," she whispered.

The other woman leaned closer.

Neatly written in black ink, there was an entry from three years ago.

"Patient transferred to long-term care. Unfit for release. No recorded death."

Below it—another name.

And another.

Dozens.

Martha swallowed hard.

"They never left," she murmured, her voice trembling.

Eliza's breath hitched. "What do you mean?"

Martha turned the page.

More names. More women were marked as "long-term observation.

Then—at the bottom of the most recent page — Katherine Ann Taylor. Observation indefinitely. Eliza covered her mouth with her hands.

"He's never going to let her go," Martha whispered. They had to act. And fast.

Margaret sat alone in the dim glow of candlelight, ink smudging her fingertips as she folded the last letters. She had written three—one to a lawyer, one to a journalist, and one to a man she prayed still held influence. She tucked them beneath a book just as a knock sounded at the door. Her heart pounded.

"Come in," she called her voice carefully composed.

Reginald entered, his presence filling the room with its usual chill.

"You've been quiet lately," he observed, his sharp gaze watching her.

Margaret lifted her chin. "Have I?"

Reginald stepped closer.

"If you're planning something—"

Margaret cut him off, her voice stronger than in years.

"You don't control me."

Reginald's eyes darkened. "I control everything."

Margaret met his gaze without flinching.

Chapter Sixteen: Beneath the Surface

The night stretched endlessly around Lily. Her boots scraped against the cobblestone as she ran, her small legs burning with exhaustion. The streets of Boston loomed around her, once familiar but now a maze of dark alleyways and looming buildings. The gaslights flickered, their glow barely cutting through the deep shadows that made everything feel foreign and vast. She had been so sure she would find Katie. But now, she was just cold, lost, and utterly alone.

Her breath came in sharp, shallow gasps as she ducked into a narrow alley, pressing herself against the damp brick wall of a bakery. Her hands were trembling, and her fingers curled around the edges of her coat, trying to hold in whatever warmth she had left. She wanted to cry but couldn't. Katie had always told her she was brave and more substantial than people thought. So she bit her lip, swallowed the lump in her throat, and tried to be strong.

The streets were quieter now, the city's usual bustle fading into a heavy, eerie stillness. Then—footsteps. Lily pressed herself tighter against the wall, her breath held painfully in her chest. Someone was coming. She dared to peek out from the alley, her heart hammering. A man in a dark coat passed by, eyes scanning the streets. For a terrifying second, he slowed, his gaze lingering in her direction. Lily's fingers dug into the rough brick. But then —he moved on. She exhaled shakily, but her exhaustion finally caught up to her before relief could settle. Her knees buckled, and she slid down onto the cold stone stoop of a shop, curling in on herself as the world around her grew hazy.

The walls of the Taylor estate stood cold and silent. Margaret sat on the edge of her bed, her hands clasped in her lap, her nails pressing into her palms. She had searched for Lily until her body ached, and her voice grew hoarse from calling her name. But there had been no sign of her. Now, she sat waiting—for what, she wasn't sure. Then the door creaked open. Reginald stepped inside, his gaze sharp, unreadable.

"You've been restless," he observed, his voice smooth, collected.

Margaret didn't move.

Margaret forced her hands to still. "Lily is missing," she said, her voice barely above a whisper. "We should be out there looking for her."

Reginald's expression remained unreadable. Instead of responding, he stepped forward, reached for the buttons of his cuff, and undid them with slow, deliberate movements. Margaret's stomach twisted.

"I have spent the evening dealing with matters far more important than a child's foolish whims," he said, rolling up his sleeves. "And now, I expect you to perform your duties as my wife."

Margaret felt her throat tighten. She had played this role for years. A doll. A servant. A shadow of the woman she had once been. But tonight, something in her snapped.

"I am not your property," she whispered.

Reginald stilled. His dark eyes lifted, locking onto hers. Then, in one swift movement, he grabbed her wrist, pulling her to her feet. Margaret gasped, but she didn't fight. She had learned, long ago, that struggling only made it worse.

"You belong to me," he murmured, brushing a hand down her arm, his grip tightening. "You would do well to remember that."

Her body was rigid beneath his touch, her mind retreating into itself. She wanted to run. She wanted to scream. But she did what she always did. She closed her eyes. She let him take what he believed was his. But deep inside, beneath the years of fear, beneath the silence—a spark of something dangerous flickered.

On the streets of Boston, a gentle hand shook Lily's shoulder.

"Sweetheart?"

Her lashes fluttered open, and she blinked at a pair of concerned faces. An elderly couple stood over her, their expressions soft but worried. The woman knelt beside her, her silver hair tucked neatly beneath a bonnet. Her shawl smelled of lavender and fresh bread.

"You poor dear," she murmured, carefully draping the shawl over Lily's shoulders. "What are you doing out here all alone?"

Lily's lip quivered, but she refused to cry. Lined with deep wrinkles, the man frowned as he glanced around the empty streets.

"Come inside, child," he said. "It's too cold out here."

Lily hesitated, her tiny fingers gripping the shawl. But the warmth of the woman's touch, the kindness in their eyes, made her nod.

The couple, Mr. and Mrs. Thornton—guided her inside a small, cozy bakery. The air was thick with the scent of cinnamon and butter, and the heat from the ovens wrapped around her like a warm embrace.

"Let's get you something warm," Mrs. Thornton said, smoothing Lily's wild hair.

Within hours, Officer Dean arrived.

When he tried calling her parents, there was no answer.

Lily was led to a small room in the station, where a plate with a simple sandwich was placed in front of her. A few crayons and a blank sheet of paper sat beside it. Slowly, she picked up a crayon. She drew herself, Katie, and their mother, all smiling. Then—she picked up a black crayon. Her small fingers carefully traced a figure— a looming shadow with deep, hollow eyes.

The monster. Her father. Officer Dean watched in silence, his jaw tightening. Something was very, very wrong in the Taylor household.

At Ridgefield, the guards didn't even have time to react. Daniel strode toward the entrance, his coat whipping behind him, his gun held steady in his hand.

"Let me in," he ordered, his voice cold.

The two men exchanged wary glances.

"You don't want to do this," one said.

Daniel cocked the gun. "I do. Now open the gate."

There was a tense pause, and then the guards relented. The heavy doors creaked open, and Daniel stepped inside. Immediately, the air changed. The halls were filled with the scent of damp wood, medicinal herbs, and something metallic. The flickering candlelight cast shadows that seemed to move, stretching unnaturally against the walls. Daniel's jaw clenched.

"Where is Katherine Taylor?" he demanded.

The nearest guard hesitated. "You don't understand," he said, voice barely above a whisper. "She's not the only one."

Daniel frowned. "What does that mean?"

The man didn't answer. Instead, he led Daniel down the hall, past locked doors, past the sound of muffled crying, past something more profound, darker. Then—the door creaked open. Daniel stepped inside. And froze. Women. Dozens of them. Some curled against the walls, rocking back and forth. Others sat motionless, their eyes vacant, staring at something unseen.

Daniel's grip tightened around the gun. He had come for Katherine. But now he knew—there were many more who needed saving.

Katherine hugged herself, her body trembling. She had spent hours thinking about Lily—whether she was alive, whether she had ever been confirmed, whether she had died alone.

"I don't know what to believe anymore," she whispered.

Ellie sat across from her, arms crossed, her green eyes sharp.

"You don't have the luxury of falling apart," Ellie said.

Katherine blinked. "What?"

Ellie leaned forward. "You start doubting what's real, they win. And if they win, you'll end up like the others."

Katherine swallowed hard.

"You need to be smart," Ellie continued. "You need to behave the way they expect you to. They don't release the difficult ones."

Katherine felt like a puppet, her strings pulled by invisible hands.

"I don't know if I can do that," she admitted.

Ellie exhaled. "Then you won't make it."

Mary-Alice approached Katherine and Ellie's small corner, her clipboard in hand.

"Assessment time," she said gently.

The two women stiffened but nodded. They answered vaguely, cautiously, careful not to say too much. Mary-Alice noted everything—Katherine's hollow eyes, Ellie's wary posture. She stepped away but met Katherine's gaze. Hold on, her eyes seemed to plead. I'm trying.

Chapter Seventeen: Shadows of the Past

The warmth of the late afternoon sun stretched through the windows of Nathaniel Aldridge's bedroom, illuminating the thick rugs and heavy bookshelves filled with expensive, untouched leather-bound volumes. The room smelled faintly of polished mahogany and wax, with a lingering trace of the ink their father used in his studies downstairs.

Twelve-year-old Julian Aldridge sat cross-legged on the floor, knees bent, his fingers idly tracing the wood grain. Across from him, his older brother Nathaniel balanced a small leather ball on his fingertips, spinning it absently as he grinned. Nathaniel had always been careless, restless, reckless, and untouchable. He never worried about the consequences of his actions because there never seemed to be any. Julian, however, knew fear all too well.

Nathaniel flicked the ball into the air. Julian watched it rise, then fall—straight toward their mother's favorite lamp. The second the leather made contact, the delicate porcelain base teetered momentarily. Then —crash. Shattered pieces scattered across the floor like shards of broken ice.

Julian froze, and Nathaniel let out a bark of laughter, shaking his head.

"Well," he mused, stretching his legs lazily, "I think that was her favorite."

Julian's blood turned to ice.

"Why did you do that?" he whispered, already feeling the first stirrings of panic.

Nathaniel only shrugged, tossing the ball from one hand to the other. "Do you think she'll care who did it?"

Footsteps sounded in the hallway—quick, purposeful, heavy with rage.

Julian barely had time to inhale before the door swung open.

Katie Aldridge stood in the doorway.

Her once beautiful face was now lined with cold fury, and her blue eyes were dark and unrelenting. Her gaze snapped from her sons to the broken lamp, and a sharp, tremulous breath escaped her lips.

"That lamp," she whispered, voice brittle as ice, "was given to me by my grandmother."

Julian knew that tone. It was the tone she used when nothing—not reason, not truth, not even God himself—could stop her rage.

"It wasn't me," he said quickly, his voice barely above a breath. "I didn't do it."

Nathaniel let out a snort of amusement. Katie's focus snapped to Julian, her gaze narrowing.

"You're lying," she hissed.

"I'm not!"

"Enough!" she snapped.

With quick, forceful movements, she lunged forward, grabbing Julian by the collar of his shirt and yanking him off the floor.

Nathaniel muttered, "Mother, it was just an accident—"

"Silence!" she shrieked.

She dragged Julian out of the room, his feet barely keeping up as she stormed down the hallway. His stomach churned with terror, his fingers clawing at her grip, knowing exactly where they were going. Katie shoved open the closet door. Her hand reached up, and Julian flinched before she grabbed the switch from the highest shelf.

Thin. Flexible. Used far too often.

"Mother, please," Julian gasped, tears burning behind his eyes.

Katie's face was cold as she raised her arm and brought the switch across his back. A sharp cry tore from his lips as fire seared through his skin.

Again.

Again.

The pain was unbearable, but he knew better than to fight. But when the lashes struck too deep, his body twisted instinctively, rolling onto his back. Her anger only grew. The next strike whipped across his face. A scream wrenched from his throat as a white-hot burn sliced his cheek. Through blurred vision, he saw Nathaniel standing at the doorway. His brother was no longer laughing.

Then—a sudden force. Edmund grabbed Katie by the wrist, ripping her away from him.

"Enough!" his father bellowed. "What is wrong with you, woman?"

Julian barely registered the rest. His body trembled violently, his hands covering his face. But he heard Katie's voice. Soft. Distant.

"He's a liar," she whispered. "A manipulative little monster."

And at that moment, Julian promised himself something. One day, he wouldn't be weak. One day, he would be the one holding the switch.

The walls of Ridgefield Asylum felt smaller every day. Katherine curled against the stone floor, her arms wrapped around herself. Her breath came in soft, uneven gasps. Her head felt too heavy, her thoughts too scattered. Mary-Alice knelt beside her, gently adjusting the blanket over her frail frame.

"Katherine," she murmured.

Katherine turned, her lips dry and cracked.

"I can't do this anymore," she whispered. "Please, you have to help me."

Mary-Alice's throat tightened.

"You have to help me," Katherine repeated, her voice rising in desperation. "Please."

A shadow loomed over them. It was Dr. Aldridge. Katherine felt her body go rigid. The doctor tilted his head slightly, studying her with unsettling fascination. Same blonde hair and pleading eyes. It's the same terrified expression. For a moment, he wasn't looking at Katherine Ann Taylor. He was looking at his mother.

"This one has been disruptive," Aldridge mused, his voice eerily calm.

Mary-Alice's heart stopped. Aldridge turned toward the nearest orderly.

"Prepare Katherine for electroconvulsive therapy."

The asylum erupted in chaos as the gunshots echoed through the unit. Guards scrambled, patients whimpered, and staff barked orders across the halls. Daniel moved quickly through the dim corridors, his gun still warm. Then—he saw her.

Katherine.

She stood at the far end of the hallway, a fragile silhouette against the flickering lantern light. Her blonde hair hung in loose waves, her hands trembling at her sides. Her eyes found his. For a long, lingering moment, they just stared. Everything around them—the shouting, the movement, the asylum itself—faded into nothing. Katherine swayed slightly, but she did not look away. Daniel lifted his hand. A silent promise. Her fingers trembled, but she slightly lifted her hand, mirroring him. Then—she smiled. A weak ghost of a smile. But it was real. Daniel swallowed hard, forcing himself to turn. He had to leave. But he would come back. He would bring her home. No matter what it took.

Margaret sat in the steaming bath, her arms wrapped around her. Tears slipped down her cheeks, and her chest rose and fell with silent sobs. Reginald had left her room, satisfied. But she felt hollow, filth clinging to her skin no matter how hard she scrubbed.

Nineteen years. Nineteen years of this. But now, something had shifted. Something inside her was breaking free. And this time, she would not be silent.

Chapter Eighteen: Shattered Minds and Silent Rebellion

The treatment room was permeated by the sharp scent of disinfectant, mingling oddly with an underlying metallic aroma reminiscent of blood and something burnt—perhaps the remnants of previous procedures gone awry. The walls painted a dreary shade of gray, absorbed the flickering light with an oppressive gloom, evoking a sense of sterility and lifelessness as if the very air had been drained of vitality. A single oil lamp, its flame sputtering and wavering, cast flickering shadows that danced ominously across the polished surface of various surgical instruments arranged meticulously on a nearby shelf. In the heart of the room loomed a long, unforgiving metal table, its surface chillingly cold and unyielding, a stark reminder of the clinical nature of the space and the fates that awaited those who found themselves upon it.

And on that table lay Katherine Ann Taylor.

Her limbs were bound with thick leather straps, cinched so tight that her wrists and ankles had begun to redden. A leather gag had been placed between her teeth, preventing her from screaming too loudly. Her breath came in ragged, shallow bursts, and terror curled in her chest, thick as fog. She had seen what they did to other patients here. She knew what was coming, and yet she still fought.

"Please," she whimpered, though the gag muffled her words. "Please, don't do this—please!"

Katherine thrashed against her restraints, her muscles straining with every ounce of strength she had left. The orderlies ignored her; they were efficient and methodical, unfeeling in their task. This was not the first time they had prepared a patient for electroshock therapy, and it certainly would not be the last.

In the shadows, a man stood watching—Dr. Julian Aldridge. His fingers curled behind his back, and his posture remained perfectly composed as his sharp gaze focused on the young woman before him. Yet, he was not looking at Katherine but at Katie, his mother. Her golden blonde hair, pale skin, and desperate, pleading eyes returned painful memories. It was his mother.

Katie Aldridge.

"Julian, please," the voice whispered in his mind. Soft. Desperate. The way she used to sound before she hurt him.

"Please, I didn't mean it. I love you. I love you."

His lips pressed into a thin line, the set of his jaw stark against the dim light of the room. His hands were clenched tightly behind his back, knuckles paling under the strain. Lies echoed in his mind, relentless and bitter. She had never truly loved him; every whispered promise had been nothing more than empty words. And yet, here she was—trapped beneath the weight of his hand, vulnerability etched across her features, for the first time utterly helpless.

Julian exhaled slowly, the sound of a deep rumble of controlled frustration as he stepped closer to the electroshock device that loomed before him. The machine was sleek and menacing, its metallic surface gleaming under the fluorescent lights. Coils wound snugly, humming with an energy that felt almost alive—a stark tool of absolute control and domination. He approached it with a mix of reverence and dread, his fingers brushing over the intricate controls, moving methodically, deliberately, as if performing a ritual.

He turned to the nurse standing beside him, her expression a mask of professionalism, though her eyes betrayed a flicker of doubt. "Is everything ready?" he asked, his voice steady but laced with an undercurrent of tension. The air between them crackled with unspoken questions, and he could feel the weight of the moment pressing down on him, heavy with implications.

"Proceed."

The woman hesitated, her brow creasing with concern as she shifted her weight from one foot to the other. "Doctor, she is physically weak—this could cause serious complications..." Her voice trailed off, the weight of her apprehension evident in the tremor of her words.

Julian's gaze snapped to hers, piercing and unyielding. His expression was cold, a mask of unwavering authority that brooked no dissent.

"Proceed," he repeated, his voice devoid of emotion, each word measured and sharp as a scalpel. The tension in the room thickened, pregnant with the unspoken implications of his command.

The nurse swallowed hard before pressing the switch. The machine came alive with a sharp crackle of electricity. Katherine's body jerked violently, her spine arching off the table. A soundless scream ripped from her throat as the current tore through her veins, her hands convulsing against the leather restraints. Her eyes rolled back, her muscles twisting in unnatural, agonizing spasms. The machine continued its work—another second. Julian did not look away.

For a moment, he did not see Katherine at all. He saw his mother writhing beneath the current, her face contorted in agony. He saw the woman who had called him a liar, a manipulative little monster, a sin. Now, she was weak. Helpless. Just as he had been. The machine whined as the current finally cut off, the energy dispersing with a final static hiss. Katherine's body collapsed against the table.

The wooden door trapping Mary-Alice rattled beneath her fists.

"Let me out!" Mary-Alice cried, her voice cracking against the walls.

No one answered her desperate pleas. Dragged from the sterile treatment room, she had been tossed into a small, barren office, its gray walls closing in around her as the door slammed shut with a deafening finality. Her struggles had been fierce; she had fought with every ounce of strength, every spark of will. Yet it had all amounted to nothing. Katherine had still remained bound to that cold, metallic table, her cries echoing in Mary-Alice's mind like a haunting melody.

Pressing her forehead against the cool, unyielding surface of the door, Mary-Alice felt a tremor ripple through her hands, which hung at her sides like lost leaves. She had witnessed atrocities that clawed at her sanity, and now they had silenced her, but it was a silence that would not last.

She let her gaze wander toward the grimy window on the far side of the room, her thoughts swirling in a chaotic tempest. She could not allow Ridgefield to claim another innocent life. A fierce determination ignited within her; she would find a way out of this prison. She would confront Julian Aldridge and put an end to his malevolence, even if it meant sacrificing everything, she held dear.

Margaret stood in front of the small vanity in her room, staring into the mirror. The candlelight cast shadows beneath her eyes, highlighting the hollowness in her expression. For years, she had bitten her tongue, swallowed her pain, and bowed her head in submission. For years, she had endured his touch. His hands. His cruelty. His dominance. And tonight—he had taken from her again. Her fingers tightened around the edge of the vanity, her breath steadying. The house was quiet. Reginald had gone to bed long ago, satisfied with himself, sleeping without a care in the world. Margaret glanced down at the small bottle of powdered arsenic in her hands. She had taken it from his study. He never paid attention to such things. Never suspected her. Tomorrow, she would prepare his morning tea. And by nightfall, Reginald Taylor would be dead. A slow, painful death. One he would never expect. Margaret lifted her chin, her reflection stronger now. For the first time in nineteen years, she was in control.

Chapter Nineteen: A Reckoning at Dawn

The wind howled outside Elias Montgomery's bookshop, rattling the windowpanes as the storm of the night settled into a bitter chill. Inside, the dim glow of oil lamps flickered against the wooden walls, barely illuminating the heavy tension between the two men standing over the counter. A hand-drawn map of Ridgefield Asylum lay before them, its edges curling from wear. Elias ran a trembling hand over the parchment, his fingertips tracing the outlined perimeter as he studied their only hope of breaking Katherine free. Daniel Hahn paced nearby, his hands clenching and unclenching at his sides. His boots thudded softly against the floor, his thoughts running faster than his steps.

"You saw her?" Elias asked, his voice quiet but edged with something dangerous.

Daniel stopped pacing. His body went rigid.

"I saw her," he muttered.

Elias's jaw tightened. His gaze sharpened. "And?"

Daniel exhaled, his chest rising and falling heavily.

"She was barely there," he admitted, his voice thick. "Thin. Hollow-eyed. Like a ghost. And—" His throat constricted, his fists curling tighter. "They were electrocuting her."

Elias inhaled sharply, his hands gripping the

counter.

"My God."

Daniel nodded, jaw set. "I wanted to take her right then," he growled, anger seething beneath his words. "But there were too many of them. I knew I wouldn't get her out alive. So I ran."

Elias stared at the map, the flickering light casting deep shadows across his face.

"You did the right thing," he said after a moment.

Daniel's muscles tensed. "It doesn't feel like it."

Silence stretched between them, heavy and unyielding.

Then Elias straightened. "We need a plan."

Daniel nodded once. "We need men."

Elias tapped a finger against the counter, thinking. "I can bribe a guard to let us in, but once we're inside, we'll have to act fast."

Daniel's gaze darkened. "And Aldridge?"

A shadow crossed Elias's face.

"If he stands in our way," he said, voice low and steady, "we do what we must."

Daniel's only response was a slow, resolute nod. For Katherine, he would kill without hesitation.

The Taylor Estate was still. Margaret Taylor moved with purposeful calm, the silver tea tray balanced in her steady hands. The delicate porcelain cups gleamed under the soft candlelight, arranged neatly upon their saucers. Inside one cup, a single teaspoon of powdered arsenic dissolved without a trace. The scent of black tea and honey drifted through the air as she entered Reginald's study. He was hunched over his desk, quill scratching against parchment, his mind no doubt tangled in estate affairs. He barely looked up as she placed the tray before him.

Margaret stood silently, waiting. Reginald grunted in acknowledgment, still focused on his papers. "The estate's finances are in ruins," he muttered, reaching for his tea. "I swear if one more—" His voice faltered.

His lips pressed together tightly as he swallowed, a sign that something was amiss. Margaret observed with keen eyes, sensing the tension in the air. Reginald set the cup down with deliberate slowness, his brow furrowing deeply as if trying to decipher an unsolvable puzzle. He ran his tongue over his lips, a nervous gesture that hinted at his unease. The room fell into a heavy silence, thick with anticipation. Then, with a sudden cough that broke the stillness, Reginald's hand shot to his throat, fingers pressing against the straining skin as if to soothe an invisible pain. Confusion flickered in his eyes, a storm of emotions battling beneath the surface. Margaret tilted her head slightly, her curiosity piqued, watching him like a hawk ready to swoop down on its prey.

"Are you unwell, husband?" she asked, her voice quiet.

Reginald's eyes snapped to hers. His mouth opened, but no words came out. His fingers clenched at his collar, his breathing turning labored. A sharp, violent spasm wracked his body. The teacup clattered to the floor, porcelain shattering on impact. His chair scraped backward as he tried to stand, his knees buckling beneath him. Margaret remained still. Reginald let out a guttural, choking sound. His body convulsed, fingers clawing at his throat as his lungs fought for air. His lips turned a sickly shade of blue. Then—his limbs jerked violently once, twice— And then, nothing.

Margaret inhaled deeply, her fingers grazing the smooth fabric of her dress. For nineteen years, she had been his prisoner. Now, he was gone. She stepped over the shattered porcelain and left the room. She would not stay to watch his corpse grow cold.

The horse-drawn carriage pulled to a slow stop in front of the Taylor estate, the wheels crunching against the gravel. Officer Robert Dean shifted in his seat, adjusting his coat against the cold before turning toward the small girl beside him. Lily Taylor sat perfectly still. Her small hands clutched the folds of her coat, her blue eyes staring straight ahead. Dean studied her momentarily before climbing down and reaching up to lift her into his arms.

"Here we are," he murmured, setting her gently onto the stone steps. "Ready to go inside?"

Lily said nothing. Dean knocked. Silence. A flicker of unease crawled up his spine. He knocked again. Louder. Still nothing. Something was wrong. With a deep breath, he reached for the door handle and pushed. It swung open. The house was eerily silent.

"Lily, stay close," he ordered, stepping inside.

The foyer was empty, but the study door was ajar.

Dean moved toward it, his instincts prickling with warning.

And then—he saw him.

Reginald Taylor lay sprawled on the floor, his lifeless eyes staring at nothing. His lips were blue, his face twisted in a frozen grimace. A slow, sharp breath left Dean's lungs.

"MARGARET?" he called, voice cutting through the silence. "MARGARET TAYLOR?"

No answer. She was gone. A soft sound behind him

made him turn sharply. Lily stood in the doorway. Her wide blue eyes locked onto her father's corpse. Dean's pulse jumped.

"Lily, don't look—"

But it was too late. She had already seen. Dean moved in front of her, kneeling to her level.

"Listen to me," he said, voice steady but firm. "We need to—"

But Lily wasn't crying. She wasn't even afraid. Her tiny hands curled into fists at her sides. Her gaze never left her father's lifeless form. Then, in a voice far too soft —far too knowing—she said,

"Now Katie can come home since the monster is sleeping."

A chill raced down Dean's spine. He studied the small child, the quiet acceptance on her face. She understood. She knew. Dean exhaled slowly, nodding.

"Yeah," he murmured. "Maybe she can."

But deep inside, he knew better. Ridgefield wasn't going to let go of Katherine Taylor that easily. And if Daniel and Elias didn't act soon—she would never come home.

Chapter Twenty: Fractured Paths and Desperate Salvation

The streets of Boston pulsed with life, even in the late, frigid hours of the night. Vendors meticulously stowed away their stalls, the smell of roasted chestnuts mingling with the colder air as the flickering gas lamps cast a warm glow over the cobblestone paths. Street children, bundled in threadbare garments, darted through shadowy alleys, their laughter a stark contrast to the dim surroundings, while the rhythmic clatter of hooves echoed off the timeworn brick buildings.

Margaret's horse, a powerful chestnut stallion, surged forward as her dark cloak billowed behind her like a cape in the wind. The sharp winter air stung her lungs, each breath a jagged reminder of her urgency. Deep-seated fear gripped her heart like a vice, squeezing tighter with every passing moment. Her daughter was out here somewhere—alone, cold, and frightened—lost in the city's labyrinth.

Margaret's frantic gaze swept across the faces of passersby, hoping for any clue, any sign. She yanked on the reins near a row of vendors, her horse rearing slightly, its powerful muscles straining under her command before it settled into an anxious stance. A gray-haired woman, her thin lips pressed into a line and draped in a threadbare wool shawl, looked up in surprise from her makeshift counter cluttered with trinkets and baubles. With little thought for her surroundings, Margaret leapt from the saddle, her skirts tangling around her legs as she landed with a soft thud on the cobbles. The rush of adrenaline surged as she called out into the night, her voice cracking with desperation. Each second felt like an eternity as she fought against the biting cold and the gnawing worry that took root in her chest.

"Please," she gasped. "I'm looking for a little girl—blonde curls, blue eyes, wearing a nightgown and a coat. Have you seen her?"

The woman hesitated, glancing between the vendors. The silence stretched unbearably.

Margaret's chest tightened. "She's my daughter," she pleaded. "She's only nine. Please, if you know anything—"

The woman exhaled slowly. "Aye," she murmured. "I saw a child like that earlier this evening. She was with an officer—a broad-shouldered man, dark coat, stern face."

Margaret sagged with relief, nearly dropping to her knees.

"Where did he take her?"

The woman shook her head. "Dunno. But he looked like he was takin' her somewhere safe."

Margaret swallowed hard, the lump in her throat making it difficult to breathe. Her hands trembled as she gripped the reins, the leather biting into her palm. Lily was safe—at least for now, she reassured herself—but the haunting fear that lingered in the back of her mind gnawed at her resolve.

With a deep breath, she pulled herself back onto the horse, feeling the warmth of its powerful muscles beneath her, offering both comfort and strength. Her heart raced, a chaotic drumbeat in her chest, but with each passing second, her determination solidified. She would find her daughter. And no one—no one—would ever take her away from her again. The resolve burned within her, igniting a fierce protection that would push her to the very edge.

The air inside Ridgefield Asylum was thick and suffocating, heavy with the rancid stench of damp stone, unwashed bodies, and an acrid odor that hinted at something sinister—something unnatural lurking in the shadows. Daniel and Elias moved like shadows themselves, their footsteps barely a whisper as they navigated the dimly lit corridors lined with peeling paint and rusted metal fixtures. The oil lamps flickered, casting ghostly shapes that danced along the walls, enhancing the oppressive gloom that enveloped them.

Their stolen uniforms clung uncomfortably to their skin, the coarse fabric a constant reminder of their precarious situation, but discomfort was a minor concern. They had one singular mission—free Katherine from this hellish place. As they drew closer to the patient wing, the muffled sounds of distant cries and shuffling feet echoed ominously, heightening their urgency. Just before they reached the entrance, Daniel abruptly pulled Elias aside, pressing his back against the cold stone wall, the chill seeping through his uniform.

"Stay alert," he murmured. "We won't have long once we find her."

Elias nodded, his hand tightening around the hilt of a small blade hidden beneath his coat. They turned the corner. A guard stood at the end of the hall, leaning lazily against a patient's room doorframe. Daniel squared his shoulders and stepped forward.

"Dr. Aldridge requested immediate patient

transfer," he said coolly, flashing their forged medical papers.

The guard eyed them suspiciously, his fingers curling around the club at his waist.

"Did he?" His voice was slow, drawn out.

Elias forced a confident nod. "Yes. He's expecting her now."

The guard hesitated. Then his gaze sharpened. Something was wrong. Elias saw it a second before the man reached for the alarm bell on the wall.

Damn it.

Before the guard could react, Daniel lunged forward, slamming his fist into the man's jaw. The guard stumbled back, but he wasn't down. He swung wildly, his club missing Daniel by mere inches. Elias acted fast, yanking his blade from his coat and plunging it into the man's side. The guard let out a choked grunt, eyes wide with shock. He collapsed against the wall, blood seeping through his uniform.

Daniel grabbed Elias's wrist. "We need to move—now!"

They didn't wait. Daniel heaved open the heavy, creaking wooden door, its ancient hinges protesting with a low groan. And there she was, a fragile figure against the dim light filtering through the dusty room. Katherine lay curled on the worn cot, her arms wrapped tightly around herself as if trying to shield her frail body from the world. Her once-vibrant hair, now a tangled mess, lay like a disheveled halo around her face, contrasting starkly with the pallor of her skin. Beneath the thin blanket, her body trembled even in slumber, each shiver betraying the lingering remnants of fear and distress. Elias felt his breath hitch in his throat, a mix of relief and anguish flooding through him at the sight of her.

"Katherine," he murmured.

She didn't stir. Daniel moved to her side quickly, placing a hand on her shoulder.

"Katherine, it's us," he whispered. "You're safe now."

Her eyes fluttered open—dull, lifeless. Recognition flickered, then dimmed. Her lips trembled.

"Daniel?" The word was barely a whisper.

Daniel nodded, his jaw clenching with emotion.

"We're getting you out of here."

But before he could lift her, footsteps thundered down the corridor. More guards. Elias's heart lurched.

"Move!" Daniel hissed, hauling Katherine into his arms.

The door burst open. Three guards rushed inside, clubs and pistols raised.

"Drop her!" one of them barked.

Daniel didn't hesitate. He fired first. The gunshot roared through the asylum. The nearest guard jerked back, collapsing with a strangled cry. The second lunged forward, swinging his club at Daniel's ribs. Daniel twisted, shielding Katherine from the blow, but pain exploded across his side. Elias grabbed a rusty medical tray from a nearby table and slammed it into the third guard's head. The man staggered, dazed. Daniel didn't wait for him to recover. He slammed his pistol across the guard's face, knocking him unconscious. The second guard lunged again. Elias drove his blade into his thigh. The man screamed, crumbling to the floor.

Daniel adjusted his grip on Katherine, his breath labored. "We have to go!"

Elias wiped blood from his cheek, adrenaline burning through his veins. They bolted down the corridor, the sounds of shouts rising behind them. They had made it this far. Now, they had to make it out alive.

Officer Robert Dean stood at the weathered entrance of Rosehill Orphanage, his navy blue coat pulled tightly around his frame to ward off the chill of the winter air. The scent of damp leaves lingered, mingling with the faint sound of distant laughter coming from the children playing in the yard. Beside him, Lily Taylor shuffled her small feet, her tiny hands tucked deep within the folds of her oversized coat as if seeking warmth in the fabric. Since leaving her home, she had been uncharacteristically quiet, her bright blue eyes still reflecting the shock of having seen her father's lifeless body just hours before.

Dean let out a heavy sigh, the weight of the day's events evident in his posture as he glanced at the imposing iron gates that led into the orphanage. The gates creaked softly in the wind, serving as a stark reminder of the transition Lily was about to face. Just then, a woman in her thirties approached, her name tag announcing her as Eleanor Ward. Dressed in a deep green dress that flowed gracefully as she walked, she seemed to embody the vibrant colors of the fading day, her auburn hair catching the last rays of sunlight.

Eleanor knelt down to Lily's level, her expressive hazel eyes filled with compassion. She offered a warm smile, one that radiated kindness and familiarity, aiming to pierce through the fog of sadness that surrounded the little girl. "Hi there, sweetheart," she said gently, her voice soft and nurturing. "My name is Eleanor. Can I help you feel a little better?" Lily hesitated, searching the woman's face for any sign of deceit, but found only warmth and understanding.

"Hello, darling," she said gently. "I help take care of the children here. Would you like to come inside?"

Lily stared at her.

Eleanor glanced at Dean. "Has she spoken much?"

Dean shook his head. "Not since… everything."

Eleanor softened.

She held out her hand. "Would you like to meet the other girls?"

Lily hesitated. Then, slowly, she nodded.

Eleanor smiled warmly as she gently guided Lily through the creaking doors of the old orphanage, the faded paint barely clinging to the wooden frame. The late afternoon sun cast a golden glow, illuminating the dust motes dancing in the air. Dean stood a few steps behind, watching them with a heavy heart, his chest tight with an unsettling uncertainty. Dean wished he could offer her solace, but all he felt was helplessness, as Eleanor's comforting presence seemed to be her only anchor in this turbulent time.

Chapter Twenty-One: Shadows of Freedom

The night air clung to them, sharp and biting, as Daniel and Elias carried Katherine through the creaking doorway of Elias's small home. The cottage sat on the outskirts of Boston, nestled between crooked trees that swayed like silent sentinels in the wind. Smoke curled from the chimney, but inside, the air was stale, unmoved for days. Daniel kicked the door shut behind them, his arms tight around Katherine's frail body. She barely stirred, her head resting limply against his shoulder. Elias rushed ahead, fumbling with the oil lamp, his fingers unsteady.

The glow flickered to life, casting warm light over the humble, almost barren space. Against the far wall sat a narrow bed, the mattress thin but neatly made. A rickety wooden table with two chairs stood beside a stone fireplace, which had long since gone cold. Books lined the single shelf, their pages worn and yellowed. A kettle rested beside an untouched bundle of dried herbs.

Daniel carefully lowered Katherine onto the bed, her body barely making an imprint against the mattress. Her hair spilled over the pillow in tangled golden waves, framing a face that had once been full of fire but was now sunken, exhausted.

Elias reached for a blanket, his hands trembling.

"She needs warmth," he murmured, draping it over her.

Daniel didn't move. His gaze never left Elias.

"I'm not leaving her alone with you," he said, his voice as sharp as the winter air outside.

Elias froze, blinking up at him. "I would never—"

"I don't care." Daniel's jaw tightened. "She's been through too much already. I won't risk her waking up in another strange place with another strange man watching her."

A shadow passed over Elias's face, a flicker of hurt quickly buried beneath exhaustion. But he didn't argue. He only nodded. Daniel pulled off his coat and draped it over the foot of the bed. Then he grabbed one of the rickety chairs and sat down heavily, his arms crossing his chest.

"I'll watch over her," he muttered.

Elias turned away, rubbing a weary hand over his face, the rough stubble on his jaw against his palm. Every muscle in his body ached from a relentless cocktail of exhaustion, biting cold, and the brutal skirmish they had endured at Ridgefield. He took a hesitant step toward the crackling fireplace, its warm glow a distant comfort against the chill that had seeped into his bones. Suddenly, the room tilted alarmingly, and his vision blurred like a watercolor painting bleeding into itself. Then—darkness.

A loud thud shattered the stillness of the room, echoing off the walls and snapping Daniel into action. He jumped to his feet, instinctively reaching for his pistol, heart racing as adrenaline surged through him. The rhythmic thumping of his pulse pounded in his ears, drowning out everything else.

He quickly turned to Elias, who lay crumpled on the wooden floor, motionless, a vulnerable figure lost in the shadows. A curse slipped past Daniel's lips, low and angry—a futile attempt to fight back the rising dread in his gut. He crouched beside Elias, his heart sinking as he pressed his fingers against Elias's forehead. It was burning hot, radiating feverish heat that told him everything he needed to know.

Daniel clenched his teeth, frustration mingling with concern. Damn, the fool had been pushing himself far too hard, refusing to yield to the limits of his body. Elias's breathing was shallow and uneven—each inhale a struggle, each exhale a whisper of resistance. His body trembled slightly, caught in a silent battle between fever and consciousness, the faintest sign of life amidst the overwhelming odds. Daniel could only watch, helpless, as his friend waged this unseen war within himself.

Back at Ridgefield, Dr. Julian Aldridge stood in eerie stillness, his lean frame silhouetted against the dim light filtering through the dusty window. His fingers tapped a slow, rhythmic pattern against the polished mahogany surface of his desk, the sound echoing softly in the otherwise silent room. The air was thick with tension, broken only by the faint, nervous breaths of the orderly stationed near the door, whose fidgeting hands clutched a clipboard. Shadows danced across the walls, flickering in time with the occasional creak of the old building, creating an atmosphere laden with anticipation and unease. Dr. Aldridge's gaze swept over the stacks of patient files; his brow furrowed in concentration as he wrestled with thoughts that seemed as restless as the night outside.

"Katherine Taylor is gone," Aldridge murmured.

The words were soft. Deceptively calm.

Mary-Alice stood before him, her hands clasped

tightly in front of her, knuckles pale. She forced her breathing to remain steady.

"We suspect a guard was bribed," one of the nurses said hesitantly. "The back entrance—"

Aldridge lifted a hand, silencing her mid-sentence. His piercing gaze settled on Mary-Alice. She did not flinch.

"Tell me, Miss Alexander," he murmured. "Did you know anything about this?"

Mary-Alice's throat tightened. She could lie. She could give him what he wanted. Or she could keep her soul intact.

She straightened her spine.

"I know that Katherine Taylor never belonged here," she said softly.

Aldridge's jaw twitched. For a long, tense moment, he said nothing. Then—he smiled.

"Lock her away," he said, almost amused.

Mary-Alice's breath caught in her throat, a sharp gasp that echoed in the sterile hallway. Before she could process the situation, the orderlies, clad in crisp white uniforms, seized her arms with firm, unyielding grips, dragging her backward with a force that sent panic coursing through her veins. She felt the cold, tiled floor beneath her feet slip away as they propelled her toward the shadowy depths of Ridgefield's labyrinthine corridors, where the flickering fluorescent lights barely illuminated the oppressive silence.

At that moment, she did not fight against their hold; there was no frantic struggle or desperate pleas for mercy. Instead, an unsettling calm washed over her. As anxiety swirled within her, one singular thought pierced the chaos: I would do it again. The weight of that conviction settled heavily in her chest, a testament to a choice made knowingly, despite the cost.

At the dimly lit police station, Detective Robert Dean sat hunched over his worn oak desk, his fingers drumming restlessly against the surface as he fought to stave off the creeping fatigue that clawed at him. The flickering candlelight danced shadows across the stack of papers in front of him, illuminating the stark, typed lines of the report. Katherine Taylor, a young socialite with a striking background, was not only wealthy but also poised to marry the heir to a prominent family fortune.

Weeks after her engagement, she was unceremoniously sent to Ridgefield, a place whispered about in hushed tones. Upon her arrival, she had vanished without a trace. Yet strangely, no official documentation existed to clarify the reasons for her confinement. Dean exhaled sharply through his nose, irritation building as he flipped through the asylum's records, his eyes scanning the names that jumped off the page. Each one told a troubling tale: women of privilege and promise, all young and beautiful, who had mysteriously disappeared into Ridgefield's ominous embrace.

The revelation hit him like a cold wave—none of these women had ever returned. A chilling dread crawled down his spine, knotting his stomach as the implications of the missing reports began to sink in. He had a sinking feeling that something far more sinister lurked behind those imposing walls. Determined and resolute, Dean knew he had to uncover the truth, no matter the cost. Something was deeply wrong, and he was going to find out exactly what it was.

Margaret stood outside the looming, gray facade of

Rosehill Orphanage, her hands trembling at her sides, the cold winter air biting at her fingertips. Through the frosted glass of the weathered window, she could see her daughter Lily, a small figure nestled among two other girls. They sat at a battered wooden table adorned with chipped paint, a single cup cradled between Lily's small hands, steam curling upwards into the air, hinting at the warmth of the cocoa inside. She looked safe, blissfully unaware of the storm brewing in her mother's heart.

A wave of emotion surged through Margaret, her throat tightening painfully as she fought back tears. Just weeks ago, Lily had lost everything—the only world she had known, shattered by the sudden death of her father, Reginald. His lifeless body lay cold on the floor, but the oppressive weight of his influence still hovered over Margaret, stifling her every thought. If anyone suspected the truth behind his demise—the dark secrets that had tied them both to his tragic fate—she would find herself facing the gallows, justice cruel in its swiftness.

Margaret's lips pressed together, determination flooding her veins. Today was not the day for reckless choices. She would not risk her daughter's safety for a hasty reunion. She needed time to devise a plan to protect Lily from the shadows of their past. But she vowed to herself that one day, she would return. On that day, she would be ready, and nothing—absolutely nothing—would stop her from taking her daughter home where they belonged.

Chapter Twenty-Two: A Fading Light and a Rising Storm

The first thing Katherine felt was the warmth. It was foreign to her, unfamiliar against her cold, aching skin. Her body, once accustomed to Ridgefield's damp, unyielding chill, now lay wrapped in layers of something soft, something gentle. The scent of woodsmoke and dried herbs clung to the air, starkly contrasting the sterile, medicinal stench of the asylum. The walls around her were not the bleak, gray stones of her cell but something wooden that groaned softly under the shifting weight of the wind. For a brief, flickering moment, she believed she was home.

But then, the memories crashed over her.

The restraints. The injections. The whispered threats disguised as therapy. The ice-cold sheets wrapped around her trembling body. The blinding light above the examination table as hands forced her into stillness. She stiffened, her breath catching in her throat. It wasn't over. It was never over.

Her father's cold, unyielding voice slithered through the back of her mind. *You are sick, Katherine. You belong in Ridgefield. You will not escape your fate.* She tried to move, but her body refused to obey. Her arms felt heavy, and her muscles weakened from weeks of mistreatment. A soft whimper left her lips as she attempted to push herself up, but even that tiny movement sent sharp, radiating pain through her frail frame.

Somewhere in the room, voices murmured. The sound sent a wave of terror through her. She wasn't alone. She clenched her teeth, forcing her body to move despite the agony that clawed at every muscle. With all the strength she could muster, she shoved herself upright. The blanket fell from her shoulders, and the cold rushed in, a stark reminder of her exposure. The voices stopped. A chair scraped against the floor.

Footsteps.

Katherine's chest heaved with panicked breaths. She pressed herself against the headboard, her fingers gripping the fabric of her gown as if she could anchor herself to something real, something solid.

"Katherine?"

The voice was deep and familiar, sending a shiver down her spine. She recognized that voice. Daniel.

Her head snapped up, her wild eyes darting around the dimly lit room, searching for the source of the sound. The flickering glow of an oil lamp cast deep shadows across Daniel's rugged face, accentuating the lines of worry etched around his eyes as he slowly moved toward her. His expression was a careful blend of relief and concern, as if he were afraid to get too close, fearing the fragile state of her mind. She knew him. They had shared laughter and secrets, once. And yet—an unsettling thought gripped her heart. She couldn't fully believe what she was seeing.

"Katherine," Daniel said again, his voice softer this time, his hands raised placatingly. "You're safe. It's over."

She shook her head, her breath coming in ragged gasps.

"No," she rasped, her throat raw. "No, no, no, no—"

Daniel stepped closer, the dim light casting elongated shadows across the room. She flinched an instinctive reaction, her body tensing with anxiety. Her trembling hands shot up to her ears, pressing tightly as if she could forcibly shut out the world around her as if to shield herself from the impending confrontation. The air was thick with tension, oppressive, and charged. A low, fevered voice pierced the silence, cutting through the atmosphere like a knife, reverberating with urgency and unspoken threats.

"...Katie..."

Katherine's body stilled, her fingers twitching against her ears. She knew that voice. Not from nightmares. Not from Ridgefield. From before. Her gaze flickered toward the shadowed figure slumped in a chair near the table. His face was pale, sweat dampening his dark hair, his breath shallow and labored.

Elias.

"...Katie... it could've been different..."

Her heart constricted painfully. No one called her that, but— The fight drained from her immediately. The tension in her limbs gave way, and she sagged forward. Her breathing was still ragged, her mind still spinning, but her body could no longer keep up with the terror. Daniel caught her before she collapsed utterly. She didn't resist. She didn't believe she was safe. But for the first time in weeks, she no longer had the strength to fight it.

The fever had sunk deep into Elias's bones. The fire in the hearth did little to dispel the cold that gripped his body. He lay motionless beneath the thin blanket, his breathing uneven, the sweat on his forehead refusing to cool despite the damp cloth Daniel pressed against his skin. His lips were cracked, his complexion ashen, waxy. Daniel sat beside him, the weight of responsibility pressing down on his shoulders. Elias had hidden his illness for far too long. Now, his body was giving out. Daniel dragged a hand down his face, his exhaustion clawing at him, but he didn't dare close his eyes.

Elias muttered something incoherent, shifting restlessly.

"...Katie..."

Daniel's gaze snapped to him.

"...never should've let her go..."

His jaw tightened. What is he talking about? Elias's breath hitched, his body tensing briefly before falling limp again. His fever was getting worse. Daniel cursed under his breath. He needed medicine. Herbs. A doctor. Something. But that would mean leaving them behind. Katherine was barely holding onto reality. Elias was slipping away. If he left, he risked coming back to a corpse. If he stayed, Elias might not have lived through the night. Daniel didn't know what to do for the first time in years.

Mary-Alice sat with her back against the cold stone wall, her arms wrapped tightly around her knees. Her entire body ached. She had lost track of how long she had been in this room, locked away with nothing but the sound of her breathing. Then, the door creaked open. Dr. Julian Aldridge stepped inside. He carried a single oil lantern, the flame casting long shadows across his face.

"You disappoint me, Miss Alexander," he said smoothly. She said nothing. His head tilted slightly, studying her. "Did you think she would truly escape?" Mary-Alice held his gaze, refusing to look away.

"She's free," she whispered.

Dr. Aldridge smiled. "Is she?"

A chill crawled up her spine. He crouched before her, his presence suffocating.

"She will break," he murmured. "And when she does, I will put her back together."

Mary-Alice clenched her fists, nails digging into her palms. She would not let him see her fear. No matter what came next, she would not break.

Chapter Twenty-Three: Fragments of Truth and Unfinished Battles

Lily sat curled up on a worn wooden bench beside the frost-covered window, her tiny fingers absently tracing delicate patterns on the icy glass. The world outside was a bleak expanse of cold, gray skies and barren trees, their branches silhouetted against the overcast backdrop, just like the stark walls that now confined her. It felt as if she had been in this sterile place for an eternity, each day blending into the next in a haze of loneliness. She missed the warmth of her home, where laughter echoed through familiar hallways, and most of all, she missed her best friend Katie, whose laughter used to dance through the air like sunshine.

The playroom bustled with activity, the sound of other children echoing off the walls—some giggled in carefree play, while others huddled together, sharing whispered secrets with knowing smiles. Yet, Lily remained apart from it all, an island of solitude in a sea of companionship. She felt like a shadow, a ghost lingering on the fringes of joy, with nothing to laugh about. No reason to don the mask of belonging or to force a smile that didn't come naturally. Just as the chill seemed to seep into her bones, sadness wrapped around her heart.

Suddenly, a soft voice cut through the fog of her

solitude, gently pulling her back from her thoughts.

"Do you want to come color with me?"

Lily turned her head, her curiosity piqued. Beside her stood a girl with long, dark braids that cascaded over her shoulders, framing a face dotted with freckles, the sun had kissed her cheeks lightly. Her wide green eyes sparkled with hope, reflecting an innocence and eagerness that was impossible to ignore. Slightly taller than Lily, she appeared to be around ten years old. The blue woolen dress she wore was slightly oversized, its hem brushing her knees and the sleeves billowing a bit around her slender arms. The fabric was soft, almost worn in places, hinting that it had been well-loved. As Lily hesitated, she couldn't help but notice the way the girl's eyes seemed to shimmer like emeralds, waiting for a sign of acknowledgment or invitation.

"No," she whispered.

The girl sat down anyway, swinging her feet slightly. "What are you waiting for?"

Lily stared at the window, her fingers tightening against the wooden ledge.

"My sister," she said softly.

The girl frowned. "Where is she?"

Lily blinked. "Sleeping."

A pause.

"Then she'll wake up soon," the girl said, her voice laced with innocent certainty.

Lily wanted to believe her. But deep down, she had already begun to wonder—what if Katie never woke up?

The ledger sat open before Officer Dean, a collection of names that made Dean's stomach turn. Young women. All from respectable families, all taken to Ridgefield, all never seen again. Katherine Taylor was just the latest addition to a long list of ghosts. A sharp knock on his office door pulled him from his thoughts.

"Come in," he called, pushing the ledger aside.

The door creaked open with a haunting groan, and a woman stepped inside, enveloped in a thick, frayed shawl that had seen better days. The fabric hung loosely around her shoulders, the muted colors blending into the dimly lit room. Deep lines etched into her weathered face framed her piercing gray eyes, suggesting a lifetime of hard-earned wisdom and profound sorrow. Her gaze wandered around the unfamiliar space as if searching for something long lost. Dean leaned forward, his heart racing; his instincts screamed that this was no ordinary visitor. There was an air of mystery surrounding her, a palpable weight of unspoken stories clinging to her like the shadows in the corners of the room.

"Are you the officer investigating Ridgefield?" the woman asked, her voice low and cautious.

Dean studied her. "I am. And you are?"

She hesitated, glancing toward the door as if she feared being followed.

Then, in a hushed voice, she answered, "Agnes Whitlow. I worked at Ridgefield for fifteen years."

Dean's pulse quickened. He had been searching for someone like her—someone who had been inside and had seen things.

"Why did you leave?" he asked.

Agnes exhaled slowly, her fingers tightening around the edges of her shawl.

"Because I couldn't keep quiet any longer."

She stepped further inside, lowering her voice.

"They don't heal those girls, Officer. They break them. And when they're broken, they disappear."

Dean's grip on the desk tightened. The truth was worse than he had imagined.

Mary-Alice was ensnared in a suffocating darkness. The room surrounding her was enveloped in an oppressive silence, a silence so profound it drummed in her ears. She pressed her back against the damp, rough-hewn stone wall of the cellar, the chill seeping into her bones and her body protesting after what felt like hours —or perhaps days—of immobility. The air was thick and musty, laden with the scent of mildew and decay, wrapping around her like a shroud.

Somewhere in the distance, she perceived the faint shuffle of footsteps, muted but unmistakable. The clinking of keys echoed through the stillness, sending a shiver of anxiety racing down her spine. Her heart quickened, pounding in her chest as she instinctively tensed, muscles coiling like springs.

Then, with a slow and deliberate motion, the heavy door creaked open, the sound resonating like a death knell. A flickering lantern's light sliced through the oppressive gloom, casting a warm but insidious glow that revealed a figure framed in the doorway. Dr. Julian Aldridge stepped inside, his silhouette momentarily blocking the light before he closed the door behind him with a soft, calculated click that reverberated ominously in the still air.

The lantern's dim glow danced across the angular features of his face, emphasizing the sharpness of his cheekbones and the cold amusement shimmering in his piercing blue eyes. A sardonic smile curled at the edges of his lips as if he relished the power he held over the dark, helpless figure before him. At that moment, every instinct within her screamed that whatever lay ahead in this shadowy confinement was far worse than the darkness itself.

"You look unwell, Miss Alexander," he murmured, his voice smooth as silk.

Mary-Alice didn't move. She didn't speak.

She wouldn't give him what he wanted.

Aldridge tilted his head, observing her as though she were a specimen in one of his case studies.

"You believed she would escape, didn't you?" he mused, his tone almost bored. "You believed she would be free."

Mary-Alice clenched her fists, but she didn't flinch.

His lips twitched into something between a smirk and a sneer.

He crouched in front of her, too close, too at ease.

"She will break," he said, his voice lowering to a whisper. "And when she does, I will put her back together."

A chill crawled down her spine, but she didn't let it show. She had already made up her mind. She would rather die in this cell than betray Katherine.

The fire crackled beside Katherine, the embers glowing like tiny stars in the dimly lit room, but she did not feel its warmth wrapping around her. She sat up slowly, the blanket draped over her shoulders, frayed and faded, clinging to her skin like a heavy reminder of the past. The wind rattled the worn shutters, and a distant creak echoed through Elias's old cottage, its wooden bones shifting under the relentless weight of the freezing air. She was here. She was safe, nestled within these timeworn walls. Yet, the ghosts of Ridgefield lingered, their spectral forms weaving through her thoughts, not so easily exorcised.

Her mind felt fractured, like shards of glass scattered across a forgotten floor—blurred, chaotic, uncertain. She had fought against the tide of memory for so long that when they finally surged back, they pierced her consciousness sharper than a knife's edge, each recollection cutting deeper than the last. She could vividly recall standing in her father's imposing study, the air thick with the scent of old leather and aged paper. Reginald Taylor, her father, stood behind his grand oak desk, his back turned to her, the muted light casting a long shadow that stretched across the room. His fingers were steepled together in thought, a gesture that seemed to echo the tension enveloping them both, heavy and unspoken.

"You are not the son I wanted, Katherine," he had said, his voice cold, detached.

The words sliced into her like a blade, each syllable sharp and unforgiving. She had forgotten this moment, or had she forced herself to bury it deep within the recesses of her mind? The memory, once vivid, is now blurred and shifting like an out-of-focus photograph. A shout erupted, piercing the air, followed by the echo of a slap that resonated against the walls of her memory. She could almost hear the cruel laugh that had lingered in the aftermath, a sound that twisted like poison in her veins. Then, amidst it all, came Lily's small, frightened cry—a sound so raw it cut through the fog, bringing her back to that dark place. Katherine gasped, the breath escaping her lungs as if someone had stolen it away. The memory snapped away with a jolt, like a fragile thread being brutally severed. She sucked in a sharp breath, her heart pounding furiously against her ribcage, each beat a reminder of the pain she had tried to forget.

"Katherine?"

Daniel's voice anchored her back to the present. She turned toward him slowly. He was watching her, his expression unreadable, waiting.

"I—" She swallowed, her throat dry.

Daniel leaned forward. "What is it?"

She wanted to tell him. Wanted to reveal that something significant had happened before Ridgefield—a shadow looming over her thoughts. It wasn't merely the chaos of the engagement fallout, nor was it solely about Daniel's father shattering their carefully laid plans. It wasn't even about her frantic search for Elias, fueled by desperation and fear. No, it was something deeper, something far more troubling that gnawed at her insides like a relentless tide. But as she opened her mouth to speak, the words clung stubbornly to her throat, refusing to break free, leaving her standing in painful silence.

Instead, she whispered, "I don't remember."

Daniel studied her for a long moment, then nodded. "When you do," he said softly, "you'll tell me."

She turned her gaze back to the fire. Would she? Or would remembering destroy her completely?

Elias had lingered in silence for far too long. His fever, a relentless tormentor, had pulled him into a hazy abyss, where he floated between restless dreams and disjointed echoes of memories long forgotten. Yet now, as the first light of dawn filtered softly through the window, casting warm, golden rays across the room, he began to stir. A shuddering breath escaped his lips, followed by a low, agonized groan that seemed to rise from the depths of his weary soul. Then, as if the morning light had stirred something deep within, a barely audible whisper slipped from him, fragile and uncertain.

"Katie...?"

Katherine's head snapped up. Elias blinked. His eyes were still hazy and fevered but clearer than before. His gaze drifted toward Katherine, then Daniel.

"She's... safe?" he rasped.

Daniel nodded. "She's safe."

Elias let out a slow, shallow breath. Then, his fingers twitched against the blanket, and he whispered, "It's not over."

Daniel stiffened. "What do you mean?"

Elias's gaze darkened.

"Ridgefield..." His throat bobbed. "They won't let her go."

The room fell into an expectant silence, the air thick with tension. Katherine felt her pulse quicken, each beat echoing in her ears like a distant drum. Shadows flickered along the walls, cast by the dim light overhead, and the weight of unspoken words hung heavily in the atmosphere. Deep down, she already understood the unsettling truth: Ridgefield wasn't finished with her yet. The realization settled in her stomach like a stone. And neither, she sensed, was Dr. Aldridge—a silent promise of the unfinished business.

Chapter Twenty-Four: Between Fear and Fate

The fire crackled weakly in the modest hearth, its feeble flames casting flickering shadows that danced along the rough-hewn wooden beams of Elias's quaint home. The heat radiating from the flames seemed to dissipate before it could reach Katherine, who sat huddled beside them, cocooned in a thick, hand-knit woolen blanket that felt more like a lifeline than a mere covering. Though her body was beginning to regain its strength, her mind was still a labyrinth of turmoil, brimming with haunting memories.

Each time she closed her eyes, the oppressive walls of Ridgefield loomed over her; the endless, sterile corridors felt like a twisted maze designed to ensnare her. The iron-barred windows, grim and unforgiving, allowed only slivers of weak light to penetrate the gloom, creating a suffocating silence that filled her with dread. She could vividly recall the icy bite of the damp sheets against her clammy skin and the suffocating press of the restraints biting into her wrists, a cruel reminder of her captivity. Dr. Aldridge's cold, impassive gaze lingered in her thoughts, his sharp eyes dissecting her existence as if she were nothing more than a specimen pinned beneath glass.

"We're safe now," Daniel and Elias reassured her

with a sense of urgency in their voices, but a whisper of doubt curled around her heart.

She had been "free" before, only to be yanked back into the shadows. Daniel was just a few feet away, his gaze unwavering and watchful, a solid presence in the dim room. She could almost feel him willing her to embrace this fragile newfound safety, to cast aside her fears like a discarded cloak, but the weight of her past still clung to her, heavy and unyielding.

"You should eat something," he murmured.

Katherine barely looked at the plate in his hands, a modest meal of bread, dried meat, and cheese. The sight of it made her stomach churn.

"I'm not hungry," she whispered.

Daniel exhaled sharply but didn't press her. Instead, he leaned back in his chair, rubbing a hand over his face.

"You don't believe you're safe," he said quietly.

She gazed at her trembling hands, a wave of guilt pooling in her chest like a stone, heavy and suffocating. The winter leaves outside danced in the wind, carefree and vibrant, a stark contrast to the turmoil brewing within her. How could she possibly explain it to them? How could she articulate the crushing weight of her despair? The moment she dared to embrace the fragile notion of freedom—an escape from the shackles of her past—it always seemed to slip through her fingers, stolen away like a fleeting dream just as she began to believe it was within her grasp. The fear of being disappointed again gnawed at her, wrapping its icy fingers around her heart, leaving her frozen in a moment of indecision.

"They always found a way to bring me back," she murmured. "Even before Ridgefield."

Daniel's expression darkened, but he said nothing.

Because they both knew it was true.

Elias lay motionless on the narrow bed, the remnants of fever slowly receding but leaving behind a body that felt fragile and spent. His skin glistened with a thin sheen of sweat, and he appeared almost ghostly pale as if the illness had drained him of all color. Dark shadows etched themselves beneath his tired eyes, which occasionally flickered open, revealing a mix of confusion and exhaustion. The crackling fire in the hearth cast a warm glow, flickering shadows dancing on the walls like specters, contrasting against the damp chill that lingered in the room.

Wrapped snugly in a heavy quilt, its fabric rough against his sensitive skin, Elias's chest rose and fell in slow, labored breaths, each intake sounding like a painful effort. Katherine sat nearby, her heart heavy with worry, her fingers nervously toying with the hem of her dress. She studied him intently, uncertain whether his occasional stirring indicated awareness or if he was still lost in the haze of fevered dreams.

The silence stretched between them, thick with tension, until Elias finally exhaled a soft, weak chuckle, a sound that startled Katherine from her thoughts. It was a sound not of humor, but one that hinted at the remnants of his spirit, battling against the lethargy of illness.

"I've been thinking," he rasped.

Daniel, who had been standing near the hearth, snorted. "That can't be good."

Elias huffed a laugh, though the effort seemed to drain him. Slowly, his gaze drifted to Katherine.

"You know," he murmured, "when I first met you, I thought you were... untouchable."

Katherine frowned slightly, shifting against her

chair. "Untouchable?"

Elias exhaled, closing his eyes briefly before opening them again, his expression thoughtful.

"You were the daughter of Reginald Taylor. You were supposed to marry a man of high standing, someone handpicked for you. Women like you weren't supposed to look twice at men like me."

Katherine's breath caught in her throat.

"But you did," Elias said with a faint, tired smile. "And I fell, just like that."

The air between them grew heavy, thick with words left unsaid.

Katherine looked down, fingers curling against the fabric of her dress. "I thought you abandoned me," she admitted.

Elias's smile faded, replaced by something tired and hollow.

"I never would have left you," he murmured. "I should have fought harder."

Katherine wanted to believe him, but every word felt laced with uncertainty. Her heart ached with the weight of unspoken fears, and there were still too many unanswered questions swirling in her mind, each like a ghost haunting their fragile connection. The pain they carried was palpable, a reminder of the scars they both bore, and neither of them seemed to know how to heal. In the depths of her thoughts, she questioned if they ever would find a way to mend what had been broken.

Daniel, on the other hand, had never been the type to sit idle or let time slip through his fingers. Yet, here they were—caught in a limbo of waiting. Waiting for Elias to awaken and reclaim his strength, the faint beeping of the hospital monitors a constant reminder of the fragility of life. Waiting for Katherine to regain her own resolve, to find the spark that once defined her. Waiting for Ridgefield, with its dark past and looming threats, to come knocking on their door, a reality they both dreaded yet sensed was inevitable.

They had to move, to take action before time slipped further away from them. Soon, the urgency nagged at Daniel like a relentless itch. He stood, restless energy coursing through him, pacing the small, sterile room. His mind was a whirlwind, already turning, calculating the next step, strategizing their next fight. Every footfall echoed his determination, a reminder that waiting was no longer an option; the clock was ticking, and danger was closing in.

"We need a plan," he said abruptly.

Elias lifted an eyebrow, his expression weak but knowing. "You already have one."

Daniel scowled. "Not yet."

But he would. Because Ridgefield's reach was longer than any of them had realized. And Dr. Aldridge—that twisted bastard—was not the type of man to let something go. He turned to Katherine.

"Margaret. If we find her, do you think she will help us?"

Katherine stood frozen in the dimly lit hallway, the cold air wrapping around her like a shroud. Her heart raced as she replayed the moment in her mind—the gut-wrenching realization that her mother had allowed this to unfold. Just moments before the heavy door of the asylum closed behind her, sealing her fate, her mother had been there, her face a portrait of sorrow and regret. Tears glistened in her eyes, reflections of unspoken words and unyielding fear, but her lips remained pressed together, a silent witness to the pain of abandonment. The echo of the creaking door resonated in Katherine's ears, amplifying the suffocating sense of isolation that enveloped her as the asylum swallowed her whole.

"I don't know," she admitted.

Daniel's jaw clenched. But they were running out of options.

The darkness pressed in around Mary-Alice, a suffocating, living thing that seemed to pulse with malevolent energy. She sat with her back against the cold, unforgiving stone wall, her knees drawn up tightly to her chest, fingers curled into tight fists as if to ward off the encroaching despair. The musty air hung heavy, mingling with the faint, metallic scent of the damp room. Time had become an abstract concept, slipping through her fingers like grains of sand; days and nights had lost all meaning in her isolation. She had been reduced to mere survival, fed just enough slop to keep her from succumbing to hunger, but never enough to maintain her strength. Yet, deep within her, a stubborn spark of defiance refused to be extinguished.

Suddenly, the heavy door creaked open, its groan echoing through the silence. A new figure stepped inside, casting a slender shadow over the dimly lit floor. It was a nurse—one she didn't recognize, with youthful features that seemed almost out of place in this grim setting. Her hands trembled slightly as she carried a small, battered tray, the metal gleaming faintly in the low light. Mary-Alice tensed instinctively, anticipating another cold dose of sedatives, another round of silent punishment. But when the nurse approached, the tray revealed something unexpected: neatly folded bandages and a small bottle that glinted in the darkness, hinting at the possibility of care rather than harm.

The nurse hesitated, then knelt beside her. "You'll need this."

Mary-Alice stared at her. "Who are you?"

The woman swallowed hard. "Someone who knows you don't belong here."

And then—before Mary-Alice could utter another word—the nurse slipped out of the room, her soft footsteps fading down the dimly lit corridor. For the first time in days, a fragile flicker of hope ignited in her chest, warming the cold heaviness that had settled there. The sterile scent of antiseptic hung in the air, but for an instant, it was overshadowed by the possibility of brighter days ahead.

Margaret sat alone in the dim light of a quiet tavern, the thick air with a scent of stale ale and wood smoke. Her hands wrapped tightly around a chipped ceramic cup of untouched tea, its warmth barely penetrating the chill gnawing at her bones. Dark circles under her eyes spoke of sleepless nights spent evading shadows, moving from place to place, never lingering long enough to draw attention. Reginald was dead, and the weight of that truth hung heavily in the air, as palpable as the steam rising from her cup. She felt the cold hand of guilt grip her heart—she had killed him.

Years had passed beneath his iron grip, years steeped in fear and pain, enduring his relentless cruelty in silence, feeling her spirit chipped away with each cruel word and callous act. Now, that silence wrapped around her like a shroud, echoing with the ghosts of her past. Just as she began to gather her thoughts, a figure slid into the seat across from her, the soft creak of the wooden chair breaking through her reverie. Margaret stiffened instinctively, her fingers gliding toward the cold hilt of the knife hidden beneath her cloak, her breath quickening. She looked up, her heart pounding, ready to confront whatever danger had dared to intrude upon her fragile peace.

"I heard you were looking for help," the man said in a low, rough voice.

Margaret studied him warily. "I'm looking for my daughters."

The man smirked. "No. You're looking for a way to stay out of a noose."

Her stomach tightened.

He leaned forward slightly. "You need to disappear, Mrs. Taylor. And lucky for you, I know exactly how to make that happen."

Margaret exhaled slowly, the weight of her breath merging with the cool night air. The dim glow of the streetlamp flickered overhead, casting fleeting shadows across her determined face. If she wanted to save Lily from the clutches of danger and locate the elusive Katherine, she knew she would have to transform—become a woman who had nothing left to lose. The memories of her once-vibrant life danced like ghosts in her mind: the laughter of friends, the warmth of love, now dulled by desperation. At that moment, she felt a fire ignite within her fierce resolve to embrace the darkness, no matter the cost.

Chapter Twenty-Five: A House of Ruin and a Fractured Mind

The Taylor estate was no longer a home; it had transformed into a hollow, abandoned relic, its silence more oppressive than the weight of the grand chandeliers hanging silently in the foyer or the intricate patterns of the fine Persian rugs that now lay untouched beneath the empty corridors. Dust motes danced in the faint light filtering through grimy windows, casting a ghostly pallor over the opulent but neglected furnishings. The servants had vanished without a trace, leaving behind disheveled, half-made beds, plates of moldy food forgotten on the dining table, and the heavy, acrid stench of decay permeating the air. In the dim light of the study, at the center of this desolation, Reginald Taylor sat dead, awkwardly slumped over his ornate mahogany desk.

For two agonizing days, his body had gone undiscovered, an unthinkable fate for the once-mighty patriarch—the iron-willed tyrant of his household, reduced in death to an unceremonious sight. His figure sagged limply, his mouth slightly agape as if frozen mid-protest, a macabre testament to his stubborn nature. The pallor of his skin was an unnatural shade, a sickly gray that seemed at odds with the deep mahogany of the desk he leaned against. His fingers curled stiffly around the chair's edge, almost as if clutching at the last vestige of control he'd wielded in life. The lingering scent of stale cigars and cold, poisoned tea hung thick in the air, a chilling reminder of his final moments.

Nathaniel Taylor, his younger brother, stood in the doorway, his heart racing with the implications of what lay before him. He had returned to Boston expecting to find Reginald immersed in a whirlwind of business deals, presiding over his domain with the same meticulous cruelty that had always characterized his reign. Instead, he was greeted by the unsettling sight of an empty mansion—a place of echoes—lacking the usual sounds of bustling servants and muffled conversation. The locked study prompted a surge of anxiety, and now, standing before his brother's lifeless body, Nathaniel felt no wave of grief wash over him. No sense of loss. Merely an encroaching unease. Reginald had never been one to go quietly into the night, so the notion that he was dead sent a cold shiver through Nathaniel. If he was gone... then someone had orchestrated this sinister event, and the implications sent a tremor of dread through him.

The old wooden door creaked ominously behind Nathaniel, forcing him to turn sharply, heart racing like a drum in his chest. Standing in the dim light of the corridor was Martha, her face a mask of inscrutability that gave nothing away. Shadows danced around her, accentuating the tension in the air. Nathaniel could never shake the unease that came with Martha's presence; she was a remnant of a life he was desperate to leave behind. A devoted servant to his brother, she had been a steadfast figure in their household—always lurking in the periphery, sharp-eyed and silent, weaving through the fabric of their lives without ever truly becoming part of it. Yet, in the moment of crisis when the rest of the household had fled in terror, she had remained steadfast, defying the chaos that had engulfed them. That loyalty, that quiet defiance, made him wary; he didn't trust Martha. Not completely.

"You're still here," he said, his voice low and wary.

Martha didn't bow. She didn't curtsy. She met his gaze unflinchingly.

"Because someone had to be."

Nathaniel stepped toward her, his mind already piecing things together.

"The staff ran," he said.

Martha nodded. "They feared what they would be blamed for."

"And Margaret?"

"Gone."

Nathaniel narrowed his eyes. "Gone where?"

"No one knows."

He exhaled sharply, frustration curling in his chest like smoke from a dying fire. Margaret—his brother Reginald's wife, the woman who had spent the last twenty years suffocating under his oppressive control—had vanished without a trace. The walls of their once-vibrant home now felt like a prison, each photo of them together a haunting reminder of her lost spirit. He could still hear her laughter echoing in the halls, a sound that had grown increasingly rare as Reginald tightened his grip on her life. Her absence loomed heavily over him, igniting a deep-seated worry and an urge to uncover the truth behind her disappearance.

"And Lily?"

Martha hesitated, then answered, "Taken to an orphanage."

Nathaniel's fingers flexed, his mind already working

through what that meant. Reginald's entire family had scattered.

But one name hadn't been spoken yet.

He turned fully toward her, his voice colder now.

"And Katherine?"

Martha did not answer immediately. The flicker in her eyes told him everything. Nathaniel felt his stomach drop.

"Where is she?"

Martha swallowed, her voice quiet but firm.

"She's at Ridgefield."

The name resonated in Nathaniel's mind like a physical blow: Ridgefield. It was a desolate place, a grim repository for burdened souls, where men emptied their guilt and sorrows, leaving behind the echoes of their failures. On the other hand, women seemed to fade into the shadows as if forgotten by time itself. Nathaniel's fists clenched tightly at his sides, knuckles white with rage and helplessness. His brother—a man driven solely by a ruthless desire for control—had locked away his daughter, treating her like a discarded possession rather than a cherished family member. The weight of betrayal hung heavy in the air, and Nathaniel's voice dropped to a dangerously low murmur laced with fury and disbelief.

"She doesn't belong there."

Martha's eyes darkened. "No, sir. She does not."

Lily sat curled in the corner of her cot, her small frame partially hidden beneath the coarse, gray blanket that scratched against her skin. A wooden doll rested in her lap, its once brightly painted features faded and chipped, much like her spirits. She stared at it, her mind drifting to memories of laughter and warmth that felt miles away.

She did not like it in this stark, cold place, where the walls were barren and echoed the sounds of distant sorrow. Dishearteningly bland food barely held any flavor, leaving an emptiness in her stomach that had nothing to do with hunger. She missed Katie—the sister who was supposed to be with her, sharing secrets and laughter.

She squeezed the doll tightly and felt her fingers turn white, a physical reminder of her frustration and loneliness. With each angry grip, she tried to conjure the comfort of her sister's presence, but it only amplified the ache in her heart.

"Katie is coming. Katie is coming. Katie is coming."

As the sun broke through the curtains every morning, casting a warm glow across her room, she would remind herself of the same mantra: "Today will be different." However, despite her hopeful declarations, Katie had not come, leaving a heavy silence in her heart. The whispers of the other children had begun, their murmurs weaving through the playground like a chilling wind, filled with curiosity and concern, leaving her feeling increasingly isolated.

"She talks to herself."

"She thinks her sister will come for her, but no one ever returns."

"Maybe her family is dead."

Lily squeezed her eyes shut, trying to block out the unsettling sounds of the orphanage that seemed to echo in her mind. The worn wooden floor creaked beneath her feet, and the faint smell of dampness hung in the air. One evening, as the last rays of sunlight filtered through the dusty window, she overheard something she wasn't meant to hear. The matron, her voice sharp as a whip, and an officer in a crisp uniform stood by the doorway, speaking in hushed, urgent tones. Shadows danced around them, flickering as the overhead light buzzed ominously, and Lily's heart raced with curiosity and dread as their words slipped into her ears.

"...Reginald Taylor. Found dead in his study..."

Lily's eyes widened.

"...No sign of the wife. The servants scattered... Someone's hiding something."

Lily barely breathed, standing in the dim, dusty room where shadows danced along the walls. Her father was gone, swept away by the tempest that had defined her life for so long. The monster that had haunted her thoughts and dreams was finally vanquished. For the first time since arriving at Rosehill, a sense of something other than fear flickered within her—hope. Hope blossomed in her chest like a fragile flower breaking through cracked soil. If the monster was truly gone, then perhaps there was a chance that Katie, her beloved sister, really could find her way back home.

Meanwhile, Katherine dreamed, but the dreams weren't hers alone. They were haunting echoes of a once-lived life, shadows of memories lurking just out of reach, pulling her deeper into their grip. In this gloom-laden vision, she found herself standing in her father's study, a room filled with the scent of old leather and polished wood, where secrets whispered between the pages of dusty books. Reginald loomed over her, his towering figure casting a long, menacing shadow. His eyes, dark with an unsettling mix of anger and disappointment, bore into her soul, leaving her breathless and paralyzed, as memories she had long since buried began to claw their way back to the surface.

"You are not the son I wanted."

Katherine flinched.

"You were a mistake, Katherine. A sickly, useless girl who will never amount to anything."

She gasped, clutching her head as the memories twisted and blurred—a slap. Lily's small voice cried out. And then—pain. Sharp and suffocating. Katherine woke with a start, choking back a scream. The room spun around her. She pressed her hands to her temples, forcing herself to breathe. She was in Elias's cottage, not Ridgefield or the Taylor estate. But the memories were flooding back, and she wasn't sure she could survive them.

Mary-Alice moved through the dimly lit storeroom with deliberate silence, each step stirring up the musty air laden with the scent of dust, aged medicine, and a foul odor that hinted at decay. The narrow space, cluttered with forgotten relics and outdated supplies, appeared to warp in the shadows. Just as she reached for the heavy door handle, a sound sliced through the stillness, halting her in her tracks. It was a whisper—fragile and feminine as if it had slipped through the cracks of time itself.

Curiosity and unease washed over her as she turned slowly, her heart pounding. In the farthest corner of the room, shrouded in darkness, a woman sat curled up against the cold, peeling wall, her silhouette barely discernible. It was Eleanor Whitmore, the only friend Katherine had at Ridgefield, whose presence in that forgotten corner felt ethereal. Ellie's once-vibrant eyes now stared blankly into the void, devoid of life or recognition, as if she had become a part of the shadows that engulfed her.

"You're leaving," she whispered.

Mary-Alice's breath caught.

"Come with me," she urged.

Ellie shook her head. "They won't let you."

Mary-Alice whirled around, her heart racing with adrenaline as she sought to escape the chaotic scene behind her. Suddenly, a firm hand clamped around her wrist, halting her movement. She turned to face her captor, her eyes widening in surprise. It was Dr. Aldridge, standing there with an enigmatic smile that hinted at both familiarity and authority. His gaze was steady, the warm glow of the overhead lights reflecting off his glasses softening the moment's intensity.

"Going somewhere, Miss Alexander?"

The blood drained from her face. Ellie's voice drifted through the air.

"I told you. They never let you leave."

Chapter Twenty-Six: Shadows of the Past

The rich, smoky aroma of burning wood is entwined with the fresh, crisp scent of damp earth, creating a unique ambiance in the cool evening air. Fifteen-year-old Julian Aldridge stood at the edge of the small backyard, his lanky frame silhouetted against the vibrant glow of flickering lanterns spilling warmth and light from the windows of the Aldridge home. Shadows danced like ghostly figures on the walls as laughter and snippets of conversation drifted through the open air, sharp contrasting against his tense silence. His fists curled tightly at his sides, his fingernails digging into the soft flesh of his palms, an instinctive reaction to the whirlwind of emotions swirling inside him—frustration, longing, and a tinge of rebelliousness bubbling just beneath the surface.

Inside, his mother was weeping again.

"You are a sin, Julian."

Her words, spoken so many times throughout childhood, echoed in his mind like a curse.

"You never should have been born."

He had been too young to grasp the meaning of her words the first time she uttered them. All he knew was that her gaze toward him was strikingly different from the warm, tender way she looked at his older brother,

Nathaniel. She cradled Nathaniel in her arms, whispering sweet, endearing phrases that seemed to wrap him in a cocoon of affection. But Julian? She rarely allowed her hands to linger on him, her touch almost averse, as if he were something fragile that could shatter beneath her fingers.

It was a mystery to him, one he couldn't begin to unravel until the fateful night he overheard her confession. It happened by mere chance—Julian stirred from a restless sleep, the remnants of a troubling dream clinging to him like shadows, and found himself wandering down the dimly lit hallway. The air was thick with tension, and he was drawn toward the echo of his father's voice, sharp and dangerously laced with rage. Each word pierced through the quiet of the house, a jagged edge that sliced through Julian's innocent understanding of family and love, leading him unwittingly toward a truth he was not ready to confront.

"Tell me the truth, Katie!"

"I cannot."

"Tell me!"

A sharp crack echoed as skin met skin. His mother sobbed. And then—the words that changed everything emerged.

"He is not yours, Edmund."

Julian had frozen in place, his breath catching in his throat.

"Julian is not your son."

Silence followed.

Then, his father's voice was low and trembling with rage.

"Who?"

His mother's response was barely a whisper, but

Julian caught the name with a jolt of recognition: Ezekiel Martin. The words hung in the air like a ghost, heavy with the weight of unspoken secrets. His uncle. The revelation landed like a stone in Julian's stomach, knocking the breath from his lungs and sending a cold shiver down his spine. The room felt smaller, the walls closing in as he grappled with this unexpected truth.

His mother—the woman who had called him a sin his entire life—had been forced into relations with her brother. She had carried the secret for years, a heavy burden that weighed on her heart like a stone, all while maintaining the fragile illusion that Julian was Edmund's biological child. She feared the devastating repercussions that would follow if the truth ever surfaced —repercussions that could shatter their lives and expose the betrayal lurking beneath their facade. Yet, deep down, she never forgave Julian for being born, for the reminder of a choice that haunted her.

Edmund shared her resentment, cloaking it in silence. He never held Julian close, never whispered words of affection or pride. Instead, he watched from a distance, his gaze cold and calculating, always ready to protect what he believed was his reputation rather than embrace his son. Julian observed it all, his heart aching with the weight of unspoken truths. He watched the way his mother's eyes would harden into icy shards whenever they met his, how her smile could vanish in an instant to reveal a mask of disdain. He noted the clipped tone of his father, who spoke only when necessary, his words often laced with undertones of judgment—words that seemed to echo the sentiment that Julian was less than human, a mistake they were forced to tolerate.

Julian came to understand that he was seen as

nothing more than an unwanted creation, a sin that loomed over them like a storm cloud. Yet, in the solitude of his mind, a fire began to flicker. One day, he decided he would not remain the victim of their disdain. If he were to be a sin, he would take ownership of it; he would transform it into something powerful. No longer would he live shackled by their judgments or shrink under the weight of their disgust. They had attempted to shatter his spirit before he even had the opportunity to bloom into his true self. Now, it was his turn. He would shatter illusions and break others as they had sought to break him. The world would know him not as their sin but as a force to be reckoned with.

Katherine stirred in the dimly lit room, her body aching as if every muscle had been put through a rigorous trial. The faint scent of wood varnish mixed with something herbal hung in the air, making her brow furrow. Her mind teetered precariously between memory and reality, wrestling with the ghosts of her recent past. She was in Elias's home, a place that had been described as a sanctuary, a refuge from the nightmares that haunted her. Safe, or so they said.

With great effort, she sat up slowly, the blanket —woven with coarse fibers—slipping slightly from her lap. Her hands trembled as they encountered the rough fabric, a sharp reminder of her physical state. Although her body was free from restraints, her mind remained shackled to Ridgefield. The memory of that chair, its hard surface pressing painfully into her back, came rushing back. She could almost feel the chill of the cold wooden floors seeping into her bones, a stark contrast to the warmth of the blanket now protecting her.

Two days had slipped by in silence—dark, restless

days—leaving her unable to fully process the reality of her surroundings. Each moment had blurred together, a cacophony of disjointed thoughts and muted fears. Had it truly ended? Would she ever escape the echoes of what had been? The haunting images lingered, refusing to fade as she fought to reclaim her sense of self within this new, tentative safety.

Daniel hovered like a shadow in the dim light of the room, his gaze fixed on her with an intensity that felt almost suffocating. She could sense his concern radiating from him, a palpable warmth, but it only heightened her sense of entrapment. She had fought too hard to break free from the chains of her past to feel caged again—not once more.

That night, as the weight of her restless thoughts pressed heavily on her chest, she slipped out of her bed, the cool sheets whispering her departure. She tiptoed toward the door, the floorboards creaking softly beneath her bare feet. The house was engulfed in silence, the kind that seemed to amplify her heartbeat. The air was thick with the lingering scent of dried herbs, a reminder of the remedies Daniel often brewed in hopes of offering her comfort.

With a trembling hand, she pressed her palm against the cool wooden frame of the door, yearning for the crispness of the outside world. Just beyond lay freedom, a breath of fresh air that promised clarity and space—everything she craved in that suffocating moment.

"You shouldn't be up."

She jumped.

Daniel stood in the narrow hallway, his arms crossed tightly over his chest, a stance that betrayed his tension. The dim overhead lights cast sharp shadows across his face, obscuring any hint of emotion. His jaw was clenched, and a slight crease formed between his brows, hinting at a storm of thoughts whirling just beneath the surface. The faint hum of the fluorescent lights filled the air, but in that moment, it felt like the world around him faded away, leaving him alone with his unreadable expression.

"I needed air," she murmured.

"It's not safe."

Katherine clenched her fists. "I cannot stay locked away."

Daniel stepped forward. "I just don't want anything to happen to you."

"Daniel," her voice wavered, "I have already been taken. I have already been locked away. What more could happen?"

The words hung between them. Daniel exhaled sharply, his jaw tightening.

"Just—please. Stay inside. For now."

Katherine stared at him long before stepping back into the house's shadows. For now. But not forever.

The sharp scent of antiseptic mingled with the warm, comforting aroma of burning candle wax, creating an oddly serene atmosphere as Mary-Alice sat with her back pressed against the cold, sterile wall of the examination room. The stark fluorescent lights above cast a harsh glare, but the flickering candles on the small table nearby softened the edges of her anxiety. Dr. Aldridge stood before her, his features obscured by the bright light, his expression unreadable yet heavily focused. He adjusted his glasses, the metallic frame glinting momentarily, as he carefully considered his next words, filling the room with a palpable tension.

"You've been quite a disappointment," he murmured, pacing the small room.

Mary-Alice said nothing.

"I expected more from you," he continued. "I expected you to know your place."

Mary-Alice lifted her chin, meeting his gaze without fear.

"I know exactly where I stand," she whispered.

Aldridge stopped. He tilted his head, a slow smile spreading across his lips.

"And yet, you still believe there is hope."

She swallowed hard as he stepped closer, his presence suffocating.

"You've seen what happens to those who resist," he murmured, leaning down, his voice soft but venomous. "Women like you—women who fight, who think they are stronger than the rules—always break in the end."

Mary-Alice's stomach twisted. He reached into the drawer beside him, pulling out a vial of clear liquid.

"For now," he said, almost gently, "I think we should silence you."

Mary-Alice's breath hitched nervously as the heavy door swung open with a creak, allowing two orderlies to enter the stark, sterile room. One of them, a broad-shouldered man with an impassive expression, reached out and firmly grasped her arm, the grip cold and unyielding. The needle's sharp tip glinted ominously as it hovered just above her skin. Fear washed over her, causing her heart to race and her thoughts to spiral. As the needle pressed into her skin, she felt the icy sting spread through her veins. Her world tilted on its axis, and in that disorienting moment, she saw Dr. Aldridge standing at the doorway. His face was calm, with a hint of satisfaction that sent a shiver down her spine. And then, just like that—darkness enveloped her, erasing her thoughts and pulling her into an inescapable void.

Chapter Twenty-Seven: A House of Silence and a City of Secrets

Two Weeks Later

The stately halls of Rosehill Orphanage echoed with the soft rustling of skirts, the light patter of children's feet scurrying to and fro, and the hushed whispers of governesses fulfilling their daily responsibilities. Yet, in the solitude of her private study, Eleanor Ward, the matron, sat in deep contemplation, her brow furrowed with concern. As she meticulously turned the faded pages of Lily Taylor's case file, her keen gaze sharpened, absorbing each detail. The file presented a stark portrait of the young girl's troubled past:

"Father deceased—Reginald Taylor, cause of death remaining a mystery, shrouded in uncertainty."

"Mother—Margaret Taylor, her whereabouts lost to time, vanished without a trace."

"One known sibling, Katherine Taylor—currently committed to Ridgefield Asylum, her fate uncertain."

Eleanor leaned back in her worn leather chair, the grain of the wood cool against her fingers as they drummed lightly against the desk. The scent of aged paper and ink filled the air, mingling with the distant laughter of children playing in the gardens outside. The weight of the young girl's history settled heavily on her shoulders, and Eleanor pondered the shadows that loomed over Lily's future in the orphanage—a place meant to be a sanctuary, yet so often haunted by the echoes of loss and abandonment.

Something was wrong.

Officer Dean gently guided the small girl into the dimly lit room, the flickering fluorescent light casting long shadows on the walls. The child's wide eyes shimmered with unshed tears, reflecting a deep-seated fear that seemed to engulf her tiny frame. No more than seven years old, she trembled visibly, clutching a frayed ribbon tightly in her small hands—a delicate remnant that had belonged to her older sister, Katherine.

The ribbon, a once-vibrant shade of blue now faded and fraying at the edges, was a cherished keepsake. Each time Lily spoke of Katherine, her voice filled with a mixture of hope and longing, imbued with childlike faith that one day her beloved sister would return to rescue her from this dark place.

Yet, overshadowing the fragile bond was a haunting phrase that echoed relentlessly in Eleanor's mind, reverberating in the eerie silence of the room—a chilling reminder of the uncertainty that lay ahead and the deep, almost palpable connection that was now teetering on the brink of being irrevocably broken. Lily's heartache was as real as the chill in the air, a poignant testament to the love and fear she bore in equal measure.

"The monster is sleeping now. Katie can come home."

The words lingered in Eleanor's mind long after they had been spoken. What truly happened to Reginald

Taylor? The mystery of his death weighed heavily on her thoughts, an unsettling question that gnawed at her intuition. Furthermore, the inexplicable disappearance of his wife, Margaret Taylor, seemed to hang in the air like a thick fog, shrouding the case in uncertainty. Determined to uncover the truth, Eleanor had meticulously requested additional documentation from the authorities, ensuring that no one could whisk little Lily away until the fate of her family was undeniably clear.

That morning, the atmosphere shifted dramatically with the arrival of the wealthy couple—Mr. Arnold and Mrs. Lisa Bellington. In their early thirties, they were impeccably dressed in tailored suits and elegant dresses, radiating an air of entitlement and impatience that was almost palpable. Eleanor met them in the foyer, her expression a careful mix of politeness and unwavering resolve. She was resolute in her duty, acutely aware that the stakes were high for Lily and her future. As she welcomed the Bellingtons, every word she chose felt laden with the weight of the secrets she had yet to uncover.

"I'm sorry," she said, closing the file with deliberate finality. "Lily Taylor's case remains under review. She is not available for adoption currently."

Lisa Bellington's lips thinned, her eyes flickering with irritation. "She is the daughter we have always wanted. We were assured she was cleared for adoption."

Eleanor remained poised. "I must settle all legal matters before releasing her into another's care. These things take time."

From across the room, Lily sat near the window, the gentle glow of the fading afternoon sunlight playing against her pale features. Her well-worn book rested on her lap, its tattered cover a testament to countless hours of escape within its pages. For now, she chose to linger in this moment, aware that Eleanor Ward, the careful and determined investigator, would soon uncover the truth hidden within the shadows of their lives.

The orphanage dormitory was dimly lit that evening, the flickering light casting long, wavering shadows that danced along the walls lined with small beds, each draped in mismatched blankets that whispered stories of their former owners. Lily sat cross-legged on the cool wooden floor, absentmindedly plucking at the frayed strings of her scuffed boots, her mind lost in thought. Beside her, Ashley Whitmore was engrossed in her own world, sketching fervently onto a tattered page of her prized notebook. The tip of her stolen pencil tapped rhythmically against her lips, a habitual gesture as she contemplated her next stroke. Ashley was a wiry girl with untamed auburn curls that framed her freckled face, her clever green eyes sparkling with mischief. She was sharp-witted and astute, often quicker than most at deciphering the complex dynamics that ran like currents through the hidden corners of Rosehill.

"Do you really have a sister?" Ashley asked, her voice was low enough that the other girls wouldn't overhear.

Lily nodded. "Katie is coming for me."

Ashley studied her, her brown eyes flickering with an emotion Lily couldn't quite name.

"Sometimes," she muttered, "they don't come back."

Lily's chest tightened.

"She will," she whispered fiercely, gripping her hands into fists.

Ashley tilted her head, watching her closely. Then, after a moment, she gave a slight nod.

"Maybe," she murmured, turning back to her drawing.

It wasn't a promise, solid and unyielding, but it wasn't disbelief, either like a delicate thread of hope woven through uncertainty. The air was thick with unspoken words, and in that moment, the space between them seemed to pulse with uncharted possibilities. And for now, as they stood on the precipice of the unknown, that flicker of faith was enough to anchor their hearts.

The moon cast long silver beams through the cottage window, illuminating the small room in a pale, dreamlike glow. Katherine stood motionless beside it, her arms wrapped around herself as she stared into the night. Two weeks had passed. Her body no longer trembled the way it once had. The bruises had faded, and her strength was returning. But her mind remained in Ridgefield. She still heard the distant echoes of the asylum—the dull thud of boots in the halls, the metallic rattle of keys, and the low murmurs of patients lost in their madness.

She thought of Mary-Alice and Ellie, her heart heavy with concern. Where were they now? Were they still trapped in their struggles, the weight of their burdens pressing down on them like a thick fog? Through the thin, creaking walls of the quaint cottage, she caught the low, rumbling murmur of voices—Daniel and Elias engaged in quiet conversation. She hadn't intended to eavesdrop, but their words slipped through the silence like shadows, drawing her attention and igniting a flicker of curiosity. What were they discussing, and how did it relate to her tangled thoughts?

"She will be my wife," Daniel's voice was calm, sure.

A long pause.

Then, Elias, his tone edged with something

unreadable. "And does Katherine know that?"

Katherine's stomach twisted.

"She will," Daniel replied.

An unsettling feeling churned within her, like a storm brewing on the horizon. Elias had been the sole object of her affection for so long, the only man to capture her heart and imagination. The warmth of his laughter and the familiarity of his touch had woven a tapestry of memories that she cherished deeply. Yet now, as she stood alone in the dim light of the evening, the air heavy with the scent of jasmine from the garden outside, she felt an unexpected shift. Once solely tethered to Elias, her thoughts began to wander into uncharted territory, exploring the possibilities of a life beyond him. The realization thrilled and terrified her as shadows of doubt crept into her mind, challenging the foundation of what she believed love to be.

At Ridgefield, the chains dug into her wrists, the cold metal biting against her skin. Margaret Taylor sat in Ridgefield's darkest cell, her back against the damp stone wall, her breath slow and steady. She had been reckless. She had gone for Katherine. She had been so close. But she had underestimated them. Now, Dr. Aldridge had noticed her. Footsteps echoed against the stone floors. Margaret lifted her head as the doctor entered the dim light, his expression unreadable.

"Mrs. Taylor," he murmured, mocking amusement lacing his tone. "A shame your efforts were wasted."

Margaret's lips curled in a bitter smile. "You'd be surprised what I consider wasted, Doctor."

Aldridge smirked. "Bravery is admirable. But misplaced."

He tilted his head slightly to the side, a quizzical

expression crossing his face as he tried to understand better what he was observing. The afternoon sunlight cast gentle shadows across his features, highlighting the furrow in his brow and how his dark hair fell slightly over one eye.

"Your husband is dead, you know."

Margaret stared at him.

"Which means," Aldridge continued, his voice smooth, cutting, "you are now nothing."

Margaret's hands curled into tight fists, her knuckles turning white from the pressure. Her heart raced, a storm of emotions swirling within her. She was fierce, determined, and passionate, which defined her essence. Yet, in this moment of quiet turmoil, she grappled with an unsettling truth: despite her many strengths, feeling powerless was not one of her choices.

Behind the sprawling, decrepit Taylor Estate, the grave was shallower than initially planned. The frozen earth had proved stubborn last night, but Nathaniel, driven by impatience and a sense of urgency, was determined to bury his decomposing brother, Reginald. This morning, he stood alone, his silhouette contrasting against the pale winter sky, staring at the uneven dirt that barely concealed the form beneath. No mourners were present, no whispered prayers or solemn goodbyes; it was a stark, cold affair. Reginald Taylor was dead, a life that would soon fade into the annals of forgotten history.

Nathaniel let out a slow, almost shuddering breath, his face a mask of stoic /resolve mixed with hidden pain. He turned away from the grave, the crunch of frost underfoot echoing in the stillness. Martha observed the shadows cast by the towering oak trees that lined the estate. She had followed him here, her heart pounding as she watched him cover the grave, sweat mingling with the cold air. A part of her felt liberated, as though the weight of her secrets had begun to lighten.

As Nathaniel walked away, his silhouette growing smaller in the distance, Martha's lips curled into a wicked smile. Hidden among the shadows, she savored the moment, reveling in the untold story that was beginning to unfold, a narrative steeped in darkness and deceit.

Inside Ridgefield, Dr. Aldridge sat at his desk, his fingers steepled before he stood his most trusted staff.

• Samuel Whitmore, the head orderly. A brute of a man, merciless and loyal.

• Nurse Evelyn Price. Cold, efficient, and unquestioning.

"Ridgefield is evolving," Aldridge said smoothly. "We need more structure." He slid a paper forward.

"Three new nurses," he ordered. "One more orderly."

Samuel nodded. "And the new patients?"

Aldridge's lips curled.

"There will always be more."

The candlelight flickered, casting shadows against the walls. Ridgefield would continue. And soon, no one would be left to stop Dr. Aldridge from expanding the Asylum.

Chapter Twenty-Eight: The Weight of Names

Nathaniel Taylor paced the length of Officer Dean's cramped office, his frustration boiling just beneath the surface. The dimly lit space was cluttered with stacks of yellowed papers and case files haphazardly strewn across a battered wooden desk. The air was thick with the smell of ink and sweat, mingling with a faint aroma of whiskey wafting from a nearby desk, where a half-empty bottle sat inconspicuously among the paperwork. It was a typical day in Boston's law enforcement, where the weight of unspoken tensions hung heavy, each moment feeling like a countdown to a breaking point.

"I don't understand," Nathaniel said, his voice controlled but razor-sharp. "Margaret Taylor has been missing for two weeks. That should be more than enough time to declare this a real case."

Dean leaned forward, rubbing a tired hand over his jaw. "I know it's suspicious, Nathaniel, but without evidence—"

Nathaniel slammed his hand against the desk. "Without evidence, what? We do nothing?"

Dean exhaled heavily. "I filed the report, but she's not considered a danger to herself or others. She's a grown woman who disappeared under unclear circumstances."

Nathaniel's eyes flashed. "Unclear? My brother is dead. My niece was locked away in a madhouse. My other niece is in an orphanage because no one can find her mother. What exactly needs to happen before you start caring?"

Dean met his gaze, unflinching. "I care, Nathaniel. Which is why I'm taking you to someone who might help."

Nathaniel straightened. "Who?"

Dean stood, grabbing his coat. "Captain Henry Calloway. He's one of the few men in this city who isn't owned by money."

Nathaniel gave a short, cold laugh. "Then let's see if he's worth a damn."

"Mr. Taylor," he said in a clipped tone. "Took over your brother's estate, I hear."

Nathaniel folded his arms. "That's right."

Calloway set down his pen. "And now you want me to waste resources chasing after a missing woman?"

Nathaniel's jaw tightened. "I want you to do your damn job."

Dean cleared his throat. "Sir, Mrs. Taylor was last seen attempting to enter Ridgefield Asylum—"

"And?" Calloway lifted an eyebrow. "A distressed mother tries to reach her daughter and fails. Hardly cause for an investigation."

Nathaniel took a step forward, voice lowering. "What if I told you my brother bribed the right people to have my niece locked away? What if I told you that Ridgefield has been committing people who aren't ill at all?"

Calloway's eyes darkened, but he remained still. "That's an accusation, not proof."

Nathaniel's hands curled into fists. "Then help me get the proof."

Calloway watched him for a long moment before sighing. "Officer Dean, you may conduct a quiet investigation. But I will not jeopardize this department based on one man's word."

Nathaniel clenched his fists, a surge of frustration coursing through him as he struggled to find the right words to express his disagreement. The tension in the room was palpable, and each heartbeat felt like a reminder of the unspoken conflict between them. Despite the urge to voice his objections, the weight of the moment settled over him, compelled him to nod in reluctant agreement. For now, he would hold his tongue, leaving his thoughts simmering beneath the surface, ready to boil over at another time.

Nathaniel rode hard for Rosehill Orphanage, the cold wind biting against his face like shards of ice. He hadn't slept well in days—not since burying Reginald, his closest friend and confidant, in a small, overgrown graveyard that seemed to echo with memories of laughter now turned to sorrow. The weight of fragmented family ties pressed heavily on his heart, a constant reminder of their struggles.

As he approached the orphanage, an imposing structure with ivy creeping up its stone walls, he felt an unsettling mixture of hope and despair. When he entered, the woman at the front desk didn't ask his name; her unwavering demeanor suggested she recognized him immediately. Eleanor Ward stood tall and resolute, her hands folded neatly in front of her like a soldier awaiting orders. Her blue eyes, sharp as a blade and brimming with unspoken authority, seemed to pierce through his facade, while her posture—unshakable and dignified—commanded an air of respect. Nathaniel felt the weight of her gaze and knew that the time for denial or evasion had passed.

"Mr. Taylor," she greeted smoothly. "I was wondering when you'd come."

Nathaniel didn't waste time. "I'm here to take Lily home."

Eleanor didn't even blink. "I'm afraid that's not possible."

Nathaniel's anger surged. "She is my niece. My brother is dead. Her mother is missing. You have no legal grounds to keep her."

Eleanor's expression didn't shift. "Actually, I do."

Nathaniel gritted his teeth. "Explain."

Eleanor turned, pulling a thick ledger from a shelf. "You are not Lily's father. If Margaret Taylor were deceased, I could release her into your care. But as it stands, she is still alive. Until I have proof of her death or a signed legal order, she remains here."

Nathaniel's hands curled into fists. "So, you would rather keep her locked away than with family?"

Eleanor's sharp gaze didn't falter. "I would rather ensure she is safe before releasing her into the unknown."

Nathaniel opened his mouth to argue, his brow furrowing with frustration, when a small voice, almost timid, pierced the heavy silence that hung in the air like a thick fog. The unexpected sound caused him to pause, his words caught in his throat as he turned to locate the source.

"Uncle Nathan!"

He turned just in time to see Lily barreling toward him, her laughter ringing like music in the air. With a burst of energy, she threw herself into his outstretched arms, the warmth of her small body pressing against him. Her tiny fingers clutched at the fabric of his coat, their gentle grip both reassuring and fervent, as if she was afraid he might vanish if she let go. Her bright eyes sparkled with excitement, reflecting the golden sunlight that bathed the park around them.

"Take me home," she whispered.

Nathaniel felt his heart twist in his chest, a sudden ache that mingled with the confusion brewing in his mind. The room's dim light flickered overhead, casting shadows that danced like his restless thoughts. But before he could gather his emotions and respond, Eleanor spoke again, her voice steady yet laced with an urgency that demanded his attention.

"Mr. Taylor, I strongly suggest you take legal action. Until then, Lily stays here."

Nathaniel stared at her, his jaw clenched tightly, eyes narrowing as rage simmered beneath his otherwise composed demeanor. The room felt tense, each breath heavy with unspoken words and unresolved conflict. He could feel his pulse quicken, a storm brewing within as he contemplated the weight of her words. This was not over; it was merely the beginning of a more profound confrontation that would unravel the façade of calm he had maintained for so long.

Inside Ridgefield's cavernous confines, Margaret Taylor sat curled against the damp stone wall, her thin shift offering little protection against the cold. The room was small, oppressive, and smelled of mildew and sweat —a place designed to break the spirit rather than heal the mind. A narrow iron bed frame stood in the corner, the mattress no more than a lump of old stuffing wrapped in coarse fabric. The single, scratchy blanket did nothing to keep the chill from seeping into her bones. She had not been given fresh clothes since arriving.

The walls were gray and uneven, lined with patches of dark moisture where years of condensation had eaten away at the stone. The ceiling sloped slightly, making the space feel smaller, like a box with no escape. At the far end of the room, a barred window sat too high to reach, barely the width of her palm. Light filtered through only during the day, and even then, it was weak and yellowed, as if the outside world had already forgotten her.

A chamber pot sat in the corner, the only source of privacy given to her. Next to it was a small tin pitcher of water, which she suspected was rationed rather than refreshed. Her hands ached from where the restraints had dug into her wrists earlier, the skin raw. The bruises along her arms were deep, marks of her resistance when they had dragged her here.

The worst part wasn't the cold, the filth, or even the hunger that gnawed at her stomach. It was the silence. She had been alone in this room for what felt like days, the absence of voices making time seem unnatural. There were no conversations, whispers, or distant cries of the other patients. Only the sound of her breathing, the occasional footsteps outside her door, and the echo of her thoughts. She had tried calling out at first. No one answered. Now, she sat still, her mind replaying Katherine's screams from the night they took her away. Lily's laughter, now a memory too distant. Margaret swallowed down the rage, the regret, the grief. She would not die here. She had failed her daughters once. She would not fail again.

Chapter Twenty-Nine: Shadows of the Past

Nathaniel Taylor sat in the dimly lit office of Attorney Samuel Prescott, a man renowned for his meticulous nature and unwavering dedication to justice. The air was thick with the scent of aged parchment, mingling with the rich, dark aroma of ink that seemed to linger in every corner, a sensory reminder of the countless legal battles fought within these hallowed walls. Heavy oak shelves, stretching almost to the ceiling, were filled to the brim with leather-bound legal tomes, their spines worn and cracked from years of spirited consultation and diligent study.

A solitary brass chandelier hung from the ceiling, an ornate piece with intricate detailing that cast a warm, golden glow, illuminating the polished mahogany desk below. The desk was strewn with an array of case files, their corners dog-eared and covered in sticky notes, yellowing documents that whispered of past trials, and a steaming cup of coffee, its surface shimmering slightly in the soft light. The rich aroma of the coffee blended seamlessly with the overall scent of the room, creating an inviting yet serious atmosphere.

On the walls, framed certificates and accolades bore testament to Prescott's illustrious career, each plaque telling a story of triumph and perseverance in the pursuit of justice, hinting at his profound impact on the community and the respect he commanded amongst his peers. Outside the window, the faint sound of rain pattered rhythmically against the glass, creating a soothing backdrop to the charged atmosphere. Nathaniel felt the weight of the moment as he prepared to discuss the pressing matters that lay ahead, the significance of which loomed like the storm outside, ready to unleash its power at any moment.

"Mr. Taylor," Prescott began, adjusting his spectacles, "petitioning for guardianship over your niece, Lily, is a formidable endeavor, especially with her mother, Margaret, unaccounted for."

Nathaniel's jaw tightened. "I refuse to let Lily languish in that orphanage. What legal avenues do we have?"

Prescott leaned back in his chair, fingers steepled thoughtfully beneath his chin. "Under Massachusetts law, a relative can petition to assume guardianship over a minor if it can be convincingly demonstrated that the child's welfare is at significant risk. This avenue, however, is complicated by the recent enactment of the Married Women's Property Act of 1855, which fundamentally changed the legal landscape by affirming that married women like Margaret retain their parental rights and maintain control over their property even after marriage. This means that her ability to make decisions regarding her child's upbringing and well-being is legally protected, creating a complex interplay of rights that must be carefully navigated in this case.

"But if she's missing..." Nathaniel interjected.

"The court requires substantial evidence of her inability to fulfill her duties," Prescott replied. "We must present affidavits, perhaps testimonies from those aware of her disappearance, to establish that Lily's best interests are under your care."

Determined, Nathaniel nodded. "Prepare the necessary documents. I'll gather the witnesses."

Officer Robert Dean navigated the narrow, winding alleyways of Boston's historic North End, his footsteps echoing softly against the weathered cobblestones, polished smooth by decades of wear from countless passersby. The cobblestones, uneven in places, posed a challenge as he maneuvered with purpose, his mind focused on finding the residence of Clara Whitten, a former nurse who had dedicated many years to caring for patients at Ridgefield Asylum.

The air was thick and briny, infused with the mingling scents of salt from the nearby harbor, where sailboats bobbed lazily against the dock, and the unmistakable warmth of freshly baked bread wafting from a quaint baker's shop. The shop, with its rustic wooden beams and sun-bleached sign swinging gently in the breeze, beckoned with the aroma of crusty baguettes, golden croissants, and sweet pastries dusted with powdered sugar. Each inhalation teased at his senses, momentarily distracting him from his pressing mission.

All around him, the vibrant pulse of urban life thrummed against the backdrop— the shouts of street vendors enthusiastically touting their fresh produce and handmade crafts, the cheerful clinking of glasses from bustling cafés spilling out onto the sidewalks, and the delighted laughter of children playing with bright, colorful balls, their joyous energy adding life to the sun-drenched streets. The scene was a rich tapestry of sounds and smells, each detail painting a vivid picture of the community that thrived within these storied streets.

The narrow passages were lined with charming brick buildings, their facades draped with vibrant flower boxes bursting with geraniums and petunias. Occasionally, the cheerful bark of a dog echoed, adding a lively note to the atmosphere. As Officer Dean approached a small, ivy-covered townhouse, he felt an undercurrent of anticipation— Clara Whitten held valuable knowledge, and he hoped her insight would illuminate the shadows surrounding his investigation.

After what felt like an eternity, Dean arrived at a modest brick townhouse, its façade worn but sturdy, with ivy creeping up its walls like a memory slowly reclaiming its place in time. He rapped gently on the weathered wooden door, which creaked open with a reluctant sigh, revealing a woman in her early thirties. Clara's disheveled hair framed a face marked by the shadows of past burdens, her hazel eyes reflecting a mixture of wariness and resignation. The faint light from within the house cast a soft glow on her features, revealing the lines of worry etched across her forehead, hinting at the weight of the memories she carried with her.

"Ms. Whitten?" Dean inquired, tipping his hat.

She hesitated before nodding. "Yes. How may I assist you?"

"I'm Officer Dean, investigating irregularities at Ridgefield. I understand you were employed there."

Clara's gaze hardened. "That place is a blight. They commit perfectly sane individuals, silencing those who dare to dissent."

Dean leaned in, lowering his voice. "Do you have

evidence?"

She glanced around nervously before producing a worn ledger. "I managed to procure this before my departure. It details admissions, many without proper cause."

As Dean perused the entries, a particular name stood out: Katherine Taylor. His heart raced.

"This is invaluable," he murmured. "But exposing this could be perilous."

Clara's eyes brimmed with determination. "The truth must prevail, regardless of the cost."

Katherine grappled with restless nights in the serene confines of the Montgomery Residence, Katherine Taylor's sanctuary since her rescue. The room, adorned with floral wallpaper and overlooking a tranquil garden, offered little solace.

"Daniel," Katherine confided to her caretaker, her voice tinged with frustration, "my dreams are haunted by Ridgefield and the faces of those I left behind."

Daniel Hahn, a man of gentle demeanor, offered a reassuring smile. "Healing is a journey, Katherine. Give yourself time."

But Katherine's resolve was unyielding. "I cannot remain passive. I must confront my parents and ensure Lily's safety."

Elias Montgomery, Daniel's elder brother and a figure of authority, interjected. "Your strength is commendable, but rushing into the unknown could be detrimental."

Katherine met his gaze, determination blazing in her eyes. "I appreciate your concern, Elias, but inaction is no longer an option."

Within the oppressive, crumbling walls of

Ridgefield Asylum, Margaret Taylor felt the weight of despair pressing down on her. The air was thick with the musty scent of neglect, mingled with the faint odor of antiseptic. She sat rigidly in a worn, faded armchair across from Dr. Julian Aldridge, whose intense and piercing gaze seemed to strip away her defenses. His cold, calculating eyes, framed by dark circles that hinted at his own sleepless nights, bore into hers with an unsettling intensity as he spoke. Each word flowed from his lips with meticulous precision, designed to provoke and probe, leaving her feeling vulnerable and exposed beneath the harsh glare of the flickering overhead light.

"Mrs. Taylor," he drawled, "your resistance is futile. Embrace the treatment, and you may find peace."

Margaret's spirit remained unbroken. "I am not afflicted, Doctor. Your methods are barbaric."

Aldridge's lips curled into a sinister smile. "Denial is a common symptom. In time, you'll see the necessity of our practices."

Left alone in her dimly lit room, Margaret watched with keen eyes as the hospital staff moved through their daily routines, their footsteps echoing softly against the sterile linoleum floor. She meticulously noted the patterns of their interactions, identifying potential allies and the subtle vulnerabilities that could be exploited.

Among them, a young nurse named Emily Thorne stood out. With her warm smile and gentle demeanor, Emily frequently glanced Margaret's way, her compassionate eyes expressing a depth of understanding that felt almost reassuring. Each time their gazes met, Margaret felt a flicker of hope—a connection that might one day blossom into something more.

As Emily administered the evening meal one

evening, Margaret whispered, "You're not like the others. Help me."

Emily's eyes darted nervously, but she gave a subtle nod. "I'll see what I can do."

As Nathaniel and Dean delved deeper into the enigmatic mysteries enveloping Ridgefield, they stumbled upon an ominous missive, its heavy parchment sealed with a striking crest they had never encountered before. The crest depicted a raven entwined with a serpent, a symbol that seemed to whisper of ancient secrets and lurking dangers. The air was thick with tension as they exchanged wary glances, their hearts racing with a mix of curiosity and trepidation, knowing that this unwelcome correspondence could lead them further down a shadowy path that had long remained hidden from the eyes of the unsuspecting townsfolk.

"Cease your inquiries," the letter warned, "or face dire consequences."

Undeterred, Nathaniel crumpled the parchment. "They underestimate our resolve."

Meanwhile, Dr. Aldridge, informed of Katherine's recovery, convened with his associates. "She poses a threat to our operations. Ensure she's silenced."

Unbeknownst to them, Katherine was already devising a meticulous plan to confront the shadows of her past and rescue her sister from the clutches of danger. The haunting memories of their shared childhood pushed her forward, while her newfound independence —a result of years spent breaking free from her controlling environment—fueled her resolve. With each passing day, she gathered information, piecing together clues and landmarks that would lead her to her sister's whereabouts, her heart racing with a mixture of hope and trepidation. Equipped with a notebook filled with scribbled thoughts and a map marked with potential escape routes, Katherine felt a surge of determination she had never known before, ready to face the challenges that lay ahead.

Chapter Thirty: Beneath the Surface

The air in the small, windowless room was stale, thick with unspoken words and quiet resolve. Margaret Taylor and Mary-Alice Alexander sat in opposite corners, their backs against the cold stone walls. The scratches carved into the surface—the desperate words of the forgotten—felt like ghosts whispering in the dark. Neither of them spoke after the orderlies, Sam Grayson and Thomas Beckett left, but the silence wasn't out of fear. It was a calculation.

Margaret finally broke it. "How closely do you think they're watching us?"

Mary-Alice shifted, rolling her stiff shoulders. "Very closely."

Margaret let out a slow breath, tilting her head slightly toward the door. "They expect us to crack. To turn on each other."

Mary-Alice's gaze darkened. "Then we won't."

A quiet understanding passed between them.

Margaret returned to the wall, running her fingers along the scratches. "Someone left these messages for a reason," she murmured. "Maybe they knew something we don't."

Mary-Alice hesitated before pushing herself to her feet, crossing the tiny space between them. She crouched down, tracing the letters with her fingertips.

"They don't let you leave. They don't let you speak. They don't let you live."

Mary-Alice exhaled slowly. "If we're going to get out of here, we need to know what's beyond that door."

Margaret smirked slightly. "Well then, let's find out."

At Montgomery cottage, Katherine Taylor had made up her mind. She stood near the fireplace with her arms crossed as she stared at the flickering flames. The warmth against her skin didn't calm her nerves.

"I want to see Nathaniel."

Elias, sitting nearby, sighed. "Katherine, you're still recovering—"

I won't recover by sitting here in hiding," she snapped. "I refuse to be a prisoner in my own life."

Elias studied her for a long moment. "You don't even know what you'll find when you get to him."

"Then I'll find out," she said simply.

A floorboard creaked.

Katherine turned sharply—Daniel Hahn stood in the doorway, his arms crossed, his expression unreadable.

"How long have you been listening?" she asked.

Daniel stepped forward, his voice steady. "Long enough to hear you plan something reckless."

Katherine lifted her chin. "And if I am?"

Daniel's jaw tightened. "Then I'm coming with you."

Elias exhaled heavily. "This is madness."

Daniel didn't take his eyes off Katherine. "Not madness. Necessary."

For a moment, Katherine felt the weight of his words. This was a man who had no obligation to help her, yet he was still standing beside her.

Finally, she nodded. "Then we leave tomorrow."

At Rosehill Orphanage, Lily Taylor sat in Eleanor Ward's small office, her legs dangling from the chair.

"Please, Miss Ward," she whispered. "I want to see Uncle Nathan."

Eleanor sighed, folding her hands. "Lily, I promise—your uncle is trying."

"Then why isn't he here?"

Eleanor hesitated. She knew the legal process was slow, tangled with bureaucracy and obstacles. But how did one explain that to a child who only wanted to be reunited with the last family she had left?

Instead, she reached across the desk, taking Lily's small hand in hers.

"Do you trust me?" she asked softly.

Lily bit her lip, then nodded.

Eleanor forced a smile. "Then trust that he will come for you."

Lily's eyes watered. "But what if it's too late?"

Eleanor didn't have an answer.

The wagon jolted violently as it approached the heavy, iron-barred gates of Ridgefield Asylum. Inside, a young woman huddled in the corner, trembling. Cassandra Jones had never been so afraid in her life. She didn't understand what had happened. One moment, she was home—the next, her father had signed the papers, and strange men had come to take her away. The wagon halted abruptly. The doors were thrown open, and two men—Sam Grayson and Thomas Beckett—grabbed her by the arms.

"No—please," Cassandra gasped, struggling as they pulled her from the wagon.

The looming building before her seemed to swallow

the last traces of sunlight.

She twisted in their grip. "There's been a mistake! I don't belong here!"

Her pleas were met with cold indifference.

Before she could fight further, a voice cut through the silence.

"Don't fight."

Cassandra froze.

A girl with dark brown hair and piercing green eyes stood nearby.

Ellie Whitmore.

Cassandra's breath came fast and shaky. "What do I do?"

Ellie studied her before offering her hand.

"You survive."

Cassandra hesitated, then grasped Ellie's fingers.

As she was led inside, her terror did not lessen—but at least, for now, she wasn't alone.

Chapter Thirty-One: A Sin to Be Silenced

Margaret Taylor sat stiffly in the old, splintered wooden chair, her back rigid and straight, a testament to years of discipline and pride, even as a dull ache pulsed in her spine. Her slender hands, bound at the wrists with coarse leather straps that chafed against her skin, lay motionless in her lap, fingers interlaced but tense. Before her, on a polished mahogany tray, sat a small glass vial of laudanum, the amber liquid inside glimmering faintly in the dim, flickering light of the lone oil lamp. Shadows danced across the walls, adding an unsettling atmosphere to the small room. Across the space, Dr. Julian Aldridge stood with his arms crossed, his sharp gaze fixed intently on her, the weight of his scrutiny heavy in the air. His expression was a mixture of concern and resolve, hinting at the difficult conversation that lay ahead.

"You believe yourself strong," he murmured, his voice smooth, amused even.

Margaret lifted her chin, blue eyes burning with defiance. "You mistake will for strength, Dr. Aldridge. I refuse to be reduced to an empty shell."

His expression didn't change. "A shell, you say?" He turned his gaze to Samuel Grayson and Thomas Beckett, the two orderlies standing at either side of her chair.

Without hesitation, they sprang into action. Margaret kicked out as they seized her arms, but their grip was like iron. She struggled, her heart racing, as they yanked her from the chair.

"Let me go!" she hissed, twisting in their grasp.

Beckett chuckled under his breath. "You never make things easy, do you?"

"Fighting will make this worse for you, Mrs. Taylor," Grayson added, though there was no sympathy in his tone.

Margaret did not stop fighting. She kicked at their legs, thrashing like a trapped animal as they dragged her down the dimly lit corridor toward the bathing chamber. She knew where they were taking her. And the realization chilled her more than the treatment itself.

The bathing chamber was freezing. The scent of damp stone and iron filled Margaret's nose as steam curled from the hot baths along the far wall. But the large wooden tub in the center? That water was nearly frozen. Margaret dug her heels into the tile floor, but the orderlies shoved her forward. She gasped as the first icy sheet was thrown over her shoulders. The water instantly seeped through her thin gown, piercing her skin with frozen claws. Her breath hitched, her muscles seizing against the cold. She tried to shake it off, but they wrapped another soaked sheet around her arms, binding them to her chest. The weight of the water-logged linen pressed down on her like an iron embrace. Her breath came in sharp, uneven gasps as the fabric tightened around her ribs, constricting her movements.

Dr. Aldridge stood silently in the dimly lit doorway, his expression a mask of inscrutability. Shadows danced across his face, obscuring his thoughts as he observed the scene unfolding before him. The last soaked sheet, heavy and frigid, was carefully wound around her legs, its coarse texture biting into her skin and binding her ultimately. She could feel the chill of the fabric seep in, intensifying the sense of vulnerability that enveloped her. Her skin tingled with an icy burn, and her body trembled uncontrollably, each shudder coursing through her like a sudden shock. The sound of her teeth clattering together filled the stillness of the room, a dissonant echo of her fear and despair. Finally, breaking the oppressive silence, Dr. Aldridge's deep voice cut through the air, leaving her to wonder what thoughts lay behind his unreadable gaze.

"The more you struggle, the longer this will take."

Margaret forced herself to meet his gaze. Her lips trembled, but she managed to whisper through the chattering of her teeth:

"Go to hell."

Aldridge's mouth curved into the ghost of a smile.

"Ah," he murmured. "There it is."

Margaret's vision blurred, not from tears but from exhaustion. Her body was losing its battle against the cold. But she would not break. Not here. Not for him.

The eight-year-old Julian could not breathe. The bathwater was murky, swirling with soap suds and the faint remnants of herbs his mother had dropped in. His small hands clawed at the edges of the porcelain tub, desperate for leverage. But the hands holding him down were stronger—his mother's hands. Katie Aldridge's voice was eerily soft.

"You are a sin."

Julian's lungs burned. His heartbeat pounded in his skull as the water swallowed him, pressing against his ears like a muffled scream. He kicked and tried to twist free, but her grip remained firm. His mother's face was eerily calm above the water.

"You were never meant to be born."

The door slammed open. Strong hands wrenched him from the water. He coughed violently, gasping for breath as water spilled from his lips. Edmund Aldridge's voice was sharp with fury.

"What have you done?"

Julian, still coughing, blinked water from his eyes.

His mother sat across the room, her hands folded neatly in her lap.

"He knows," she said softly.

Edmund's fingers tightened on Julian's shoulders. "Knows what?"

Katie's eyes were empty.

"That he is a sin."

Julian felt his father's grip begin to slip, fingers trembling as if they were surrendering to the weight of despair. His lungs burned fiercely, the sharp, stinging sensation deepening with each desperate gasp for air. Water clung to his skin, droplets cascading down like relentless rain, chilling him to the bone. But more suffocating than the cold was the heaviness of those words—sharp and accusatory—settling over him like a dark shroud, wrapping him in a fog of grief and regret, dragging him further into the depths of a second drowning.

The Rosehill Orphanage dormitory lay cloaked in heavy silence, broken only by the occasional creak of aging wooden bedframes and the soft, rhythmic breathing of sleeping children scattered throughout the dimly lit room. In the far corner, beneath a threadbare, thin blanket, Lily Taylor was wide awake, her heart racing in the stillness. She lay curled up in a tight ball, her small hands gripping the frayed fabric as if it could shield her from the memories that clawed at the edges of her mind.

Tonight, she wasn't drifting into sleep; she was resisting it, caught in a vivid recollection that had seeped through the cracks of her consciousness. The shadowy corridors of her former home loomed in her thoughts—long forgotten, yet painfully vivid. She could almost hear her father's voice echoing down the hall, a thunderous growl of anger that sent shivers racing down her spine. It was the voice that had filled their modest house with fear, a sound that twisted the air into something suffocating.

His glare had been piercing, a silent storm that raged beneath a facade of calm. There was no warmth in his eyes, only a chilling emptiness that sent a message stronger than words ever could—it was a look that spoke of disappointment and indifference intertwined, a void that was somehow worse than hatred. Trembling, Lily squeezed her eyes shut tighter, trying to ward off the whispers that lingered, a cacophony of names and words that floated through her mind, haunting her in the heavy darkness.

"Katie isn't coming back for you."

A sob caught in her throat.

She rolled onto her side, wishing for the familiar warmth of her sister's arms wrapped around her. She longed for Katherine's soft lullabies, the gentle cadence of her voice that always seemed to chase away the shadows of the night. She remembered how Katherine would brush her hair with careful strokes, weaving stories of distant lands filled with wonders, vibrant cities, and magical realms, far beyond the confines of the sprawling

Taylor estate. But now, as the coldness of the empty room seeped into her bones, Lily felt the absence of her sister like a heavy weight upon her chest. Katherine wasn't here, and with each passing day, the hope that she ever felt more like a distant dream. A single tear slipped down her cheek, glistening in the dim light. She whispered against the pillow, her voice barely audible, as she confided her loneliness to the darkened corners of the room, so softly that only she could hear the ache of her heart.

"Please, Katie... come back."

Nathaniel slowly sipped his amber whiskey at the polished mahogany bar of the Taylor Estate, the dim light casting a warm glow on his contemplative face. He finally set the glass down, its contents swirling like his thoughts. "She's at Rosehill Orphanage," he said, his voice laced with a mix of resignation and concern.

Katherine felt a knot tighten in her stomach at the mention of the orphanage. Rosehill was a somber place, a home for the forgotten where laughter was a distant memory, and hope flickered like a candle in the wind. It was a sanctuary for children without guardians, hidden away from the bustling world outside, where their fates hung in a precarious balance. Each child carried a story, and in that silence, their dreams often fell into shadows, waiting for a chance to be seen.

She shook her head. "She can't stay there."

"I know," Nathaniel said, his voice steady. "But we have to be careful, Katherine. You're still a minor. You can't claim her."

Katherine's fingernails dug into her palms.

"So, what do we do?" she whispered.

Nathaniel's expression was unreadable.

"We find a way to bring her home," he said. "Legally, if we can. Otherwise…"

He exhaled sharply, setting his drink aside.

"I will get her back."

Katherine studied his face intently, noting the way the light from the flickering candle danced across his features, casting shadows that softened his sharp jawline. The deep lines etched around his eyes told stories of struggle and perseverance, but for the first time, she wasn't afraid of the man sitting across from her. Instead, a sense of calm washed over her, and she found herself believing in him, in the sincerity of his expression and the strength behind his gaze. It was as if the weight of their shared past had lifted, allowing her to see him clearly without the fog of doubt.

Chapter Thirty-Two: A Choice of Power and Love

The Taylor estate remained unchanged, its exterior stoic against the passage of time. But Katherine had transformed during her years away. As she stepped through the heavy oak door, a familiar blend of polished mahogany, the sweet scent of candle wax, and the faint, haunting aroma of lingering tobacco smoke enveloped her, just as it had since childhood. The interior was a snapshot of the past, as if time had frozen while she was gone.

Every surface gleamed with meticulous care, and the walls, lined with faded family photographs, stood as silent witnesses to a history that now felt distant. Yet, despite the house's pristine condition, the warmth she once felt as a child was starkly absent. It was as if the very walls were aware of her betrayal, reflecting the heartache she had endured.

As she wandered through the dimly lit corridors, the air thick with unspoken memories, she could almost hear the echoes of past conversations resonating around her. Her father's harsh, unwavering commands reverberated in her mind, a constant reminder of his iron grip. Meanwhile, her mother's quiet, resigned sighs painted a backdrop of subdued despair, while Lily's bright laughter—once a melody that filled every corner—now rang only in the shadows, silenced by the weight of what had transpired.

Katherine's fingers curled into fists at her sides, her resolve hardening like steel. She would bring her sister home from the darkness that had consumed their lives, and she would confront anyone who dared to keep them apart again. Nothing would stand in her way; she was determined to reclaim the laughter that had once brightened their world.

She reached the parlor, where a single lamp cast a golden glow over the familiar space. And there, standing by the window, was Martha. The woman turned at the sound of Katherine's footsteps, her sharp blue eyes widening in disbelief. Then, in an instant, she rushed forward, wrapping Katherine in a fierce embrace.

"Katie..." Martha's voice trembled, her hands gripping Katherine as if afraid she might vanish.

Katherine shuddered, her throat tightening as she clung to the one person who had never turned her away.

"I thought I had lost you," Martha whispered.

Katherine swallowed hard. "I thought I had lost you too."

Martha pulled back just enough to cup Katherine's face in her weathered hands. She studied her, her expression shifting from relief to heartbreak.

"You're thinner," she murmured. "Your eyes... they don't look like yours anymore."

Katherine tried to smile, but it faltered. "I've seen too much."

Martha nodded solemnly, her touch lingering a moment longer before she led Katherine to the settee by the window. The silence stretched, warm yet weighted.

Then, Martha asked quietly, "What do you need

from me, child?"

Katherine exhaled, steadying herself. "I need to bring Lily home."

Martha reached for her hands, gripping them tightly.

"Then we will bring her home."

Katherine's breath hitched. "I have no rights to her."

"She is scared, Katie," Martha said, voice thick with emotion. "I see it in her eyes when I visit her."

Katherine stared. "You've been to see her?"

Martha nodded. "Of course. I could not leave her alone in that place without someone who knows her."

Tears blurred Katherine's vision. For weeks, she had felt like she was fighting this battle alone. But Martha had been watching over Lily. Protecting her.

"Thank you," Katherine whispered, gripping Martha's hands harder.

Martha's eyes shone with quiet determination. "You have always been the one protecting Lily. Now, let me help protect you both."

Katherine exhaled shakily. She had endured Ridgefield, suffered cruelty, survived betrayal. But Lily had endured something, too. The loss of a sister, the confusion of abandonment, the loneliness of an orphanage.

"I will do whatever it takes," Katherine vowed.

Martha nodded knowingly. "You already know what you need to do, don't you?"

Katherine hesitated. She did. She already knew the answer.

The Montgomery cottage felt empty, suffocating in its quiet. Elias sat in the back room of the bookshop, a half-empty bottle of whiskey beside him, his hands clasped over his face. Katherine was gone. Not just taken. Not just lost. But choosing another man. For days, he had told himself he should be grateful she was safe. That it didn't matter if she was with someone else. That he had never had the right to claim her in the first place. But it was a lie. She had been his reason to keep fighting. His reason to keep searching. His reason to believe in something more than the small, stagnant life he had been forced into. And now? She was slipping away. The memory of her haunted him—her smile, her laughter, the way she had once looked at him like he was her world. Daniel had stolen that from him. No—he had given it away. The door creaked open. He didn't need to look up. Daniel.

Elias scoffed, swirling the whiskey in his glass. "Come to gloat?"

Daniel stepped inside, arms crossed, his posture tense. "No."

Elias took a slow sip. "Then what do you want?"

Daniel exhaled through his nose. "To see if you're still capable of fighting for something."

Elias laughed bitterly. "Fighting for what? For her?" His grip tightened around the glass. "Looks like you've already won."

Daniel's jaw twitched. "Is that what you think this is? A competition?"

Elias slammed the glass onto the table. "It was never a competition. Because I never had a chance, did I?"

Daniel held his gaze, unwavering.

"I didn't steal her from you," Daniel said. "You let her go."

Elias flinched.

Daniel stepped closer. "If you truly love her, you'd

want what's best for her."

Elias' eyes darkened. "And that's you?"

Daniel didn't blink. "Yes."

Elias pushed up from his chair. "And what if I told you she doesn't love you?"

Daniel hesitated for only a moment.

"Then I'll give her every reason to stay."

The words hung between them, heavy with finality. Elias looked away first. He had already lost.

Daniel exhaled, his voice quieter this time. "This isn't over."

Elias didn't answer. Because he knew Daniel was right.

Meanwhile at Ridgefield… Margaret remained in isolation, the cold seeping into her bones long after the wet sheets had been removed. The nurses ignored her pleas for warmth, their eyes vacant as they followed orders without question. Dr. Aldridge watched from his office window as she was dragged back to her cell, her body weak from the treatment, her spirit still unbroken.

Mary-Alice attempted to visit Margaret that afternoon, but her request was denied. The orderly at the desk barely looked up as he told her, "Dr. Aldridge has restricted access. No exceptions." Fury bubbled in Mary-Alice's chest. She knew what this meant—Margaret was being kept quiet.

On the women's ward, Ellie sat beside Cassandra Jones, the newest patient, watching as the young woman's head lolled to the side. The morphine had taken full effect, her eyelids fluttering as she mumbled something incoherent. Ellie clenched her fists, her voice a whisper. "I tried to warn you…"

But no one ever listened in time.

That night, as Katherine sat in the quiet of the Taylor estate, Nathaniel received a letter. The wax seal was broken. The parchment was yellowed. But the words written in ink were clear and urgent.

"Be careful who you trust. Ridgefield's secrets run deeper than you know."

Nathaniel's breath hitched. Who sent this? And what did it mean?

Chapter Thirty-Three: Bound by Vows, Driven by Purpose

March 1856

The frigid March air sliced through Katherine's clothing like a thousand icy needles as she stepped down from the plush velvet-lined carriage, its wheels sinking slightly into the muddy street. The towering, weathered stone walls of Boston's city clerk's office loomed over her, their ancient architecture casting long, ominous shadows that stretched across the cobblestone pavement. Just a week ago, she had been a prisoner in the oppressive confines of Ridgefield, shackled by both iron and despair. Now, standing resolutely before the heavy oak door adorned with brass fittings, she felt the weight of the possibility pressing down on her. This door, she knew, held the power to shape her destiny. Drawing in a deep, trembling breath, she steeled herself for what lay ahead, the determination to reclaim her life igniting a fervent ember within her chest.

Nathaniel stood beside her, his posture rigid and unwavering, embodying the protective presence she hadn't realized she needed until this very moment. The sunlight filtered through the tall windows of the courtroom, casting a warm glow on his determined features. He had meticulously signed the papers earlier, assuming legal guardianship with a sense of responsibility that was palpable in the air. His voice, steady and resolute, had echoed in her mind as he vouchsafed her rights amidst the flutter of emotions surrounding them. With each passing second, she felt the weight of his name—a name that held undeniable power and credibility in this setting—and today, as she faced an uncertain future, she found solace in knowing that she was not alone.

Daniel stepped up to her side, his tailored coat sharp against the fading twilight. The fabric glimmered slightly, a deep navy that contrasted with the rich autumn hues surrounding them. His jaw was set in quiet determination, a subtle muscle twitch revealing the intensity of his focus. She had known him for barely three weeks, but in that short time, he had proven himself a steadfast ally, ready to face whatever challenges lay ahead. As they stood together, she could sense the quiet strength emanating from him, providing an unexpected sense of comfort amidst the uncertainty.

Inside, the city clerk eyed them with mild curiosity as they approached. "Marriage license?"

Katherine nodded, her fingers tightening around her gloves.

The clerk flipped open his registry. "You've already filed your intention to marry. Today, we issued the license. I need the guardian's final confirmation." His gaze shifted to Nathaniel.

"I am Katherine's next of kin," Nathaniel said firmly, sliding the signed document across the desk. "And I consent to this marriage."

The clerk examined the paper, his pen scratching against the form. "Very well. The law requires a brief waiting period before the ceremony, but given your circumstances, an officiant can perform the wedding as soon as tomorrow."

Katherine's stomach was knotted with anxiety as she sat on the edge of the bed, staring at the wall painted a muted blue that felt confining. Tomorrow was the day. This was really happening. She remembered the dream she once had of marriage—a love match, full of warmth and laughter that echoed through a cozy home, where every choice could be mutually made between soulmates. But life, with its unpredictable twists, had carved a different path for her—a path lined with responsibility and resignation.

Her gaze flickered to Daniel, who stood across the room, tall and steady, with an expression that was an uneasy mix of determination and patience. He was dressed in a crisp white shirt, the sleeves rolled up to his elbows, revealing forearms that had grown accustomed to labor. In that moment, he looked like the anchor she didn't know she needed, offering her the only thing she had left—a way forward, however uncertain it was. As she took a deep breath, she felt the weight of her choice loom over her, a heavy mixture of hope and trepidation swirling in her chest.

The clerk stamped the document. "You'll need two witnesses and a minister or justice of the peace. Do you have arrangements?"

Nathaniel gave a curt nod. "A minister will perform the ceremony. Martha and I will serve as witnesses."

Daniel turned to Katherine, his voice low. "Are you certain this is what you want?"

A heavy silence enveloped the room, punctuated only by the faint crackle of the dying fire. No. She wanted her father alive—not as the cruel, monstrous figure who had terrorized her childhood, but as the warm, loving dad he should have been, the one who would have lifted her high on his shoulders and spun her around in joyous laughter. She longed for her mother to return, not as the ghostly silhouette lost to the dark depths of madness and grief, but as the nurturing woman who once filled their home with warmth and the scent of fresh-baked bread. She ached for Lily, her little sister, to be safe in her arms instead of alone and vulnerable in a cold, unfamiliar orphanage where shadows lingered longer than the light. Yet, as the weight of reality pressed down on her heart, she realized that her deepest desires no longer mattered. What mattered now was survival—finding a way to navigate the cruel world that had stripped her of everything she held dear.

She lifted her chin. "Yes."

The clerk slid the marriage license across the desk. "Then, Miss Taylor, Mr. Hahn—congratulations. You are cleared to wed."

At the sprawling Taylor estate, Katherine found little time to gather her thoughts as an unexpected visitor made his entrance. Elias loomed in the doorway, his silhouette framed by the dim light of the late afternoon. The mist that clung to the air had settled on his dark coat, causing it to glisten slightly as droplets clung to the fabric, emphasizing the chill of the day. Shadowed eyes, filled with a mix of urgency and uncertainty, met Katherine's gaze, hinting at unspoken troubles waiting to unfold.

Martha frowned. "Mr. Montgomery, now is not the time—"

"Let him in," Katherine said, surprising herself.

He stepped inside, shaking off the cold. He looked at her like she had been stolen from him.

"You're marrying him?" His voice was rough, edged with something unreadable.

Katherine felt Martha and Nathaniel watching, waiting for her response. She squared her shoulders. "Yes."

Elias exhaled sharply, raking a hand through his hair. He took a step closer. "Katherine, I know you think this is your only choice, but it's not."

Her heart pounded. Daniel had been nothing but patient, kind, and protective. But Elias... Elias had been her dream before her life unraveled.

She forced herself to speak. "Do you have another solution?"

He hesitated. The silence was her answer.

Her throat tightened, but her voice did not waver. "Then it's already decided."

Elias looked at her honestly as if trying to memorize her face before she was lost to him forever.

His jaw clenched. "I hope he deserves you."

Without another word, he turned sharply on his heel and strode out the door, his footsteps echoing against the wooden floor. Katherine stood still, her heart pounding in her chest, rooted to the spot as she watched the door swing slowly shut behind him, its heavy frame thudding softly in place. The air felt thick with unspoken words, and she couldn't shake the sense of finality that lingered in the room, tightening around her like a vice.

Meanwhile, at Ridgefield Asylum, the corridors were unnaturally silent, an eerie stillness settling over the usually bustling institution. Dr. Aldridge stood in his cramped office, meticulously tapping his fingers against the polished oak desk, creating a rhythmic sound that contrasted sharply with the unsettling quiet surrounding him. A solitary oil lamp flickered weakly in the dim light, casting elongated shadows that curled and danced across stacks of paperwork. An unsettling feeling coiled in his gut; something was amiss.

Margaret Taylor had been confined to isolation after vehemently resisting her prescribed medication—her refusal was not merely rebellious; it was desperate. Under his directives, she had been subjected to the harsh regimen of cold sheet therapy, a treatment designed to shock the mind and body into submission. And yet—she was gone. The neatly made bed in the isolation room lay empty, the pristine sheets undisturbed except for the dark marks where her restraints had previously been tightly fastened. Panic surged within Aldridge as he realized that someone had aided her escape.

His urgent gaze swept across the nurses' logs sprawled across his desk, scrutinizing each entry for clues: a name, a lost moment in time, a procedural error. But there were no errors—only the undeniable fact of a missing woman who had eluded him. His fist tightened around his pen, and as he pressed it onto the paper, a dark inkblot blossomed, an accidental emblem of his growing frustration. Deep down, he knew she wouldn't get far. But the uncertainty gnawed at him like an unrelenting shadow. He had to act swiftly; the stakes had just been raised.

The wind howled against the stone walls of Rosehill Orphanage as Lily slipped out the back door, her breath forming small clouds in the bitter night air. She had waited long enough. She had watched Eleanor Ward tuck the other girls into bed and waited for the matron's footsteps to fade down the hall. When she was confident the coast was clear, she crept to the kitchen and unlatched the servant's entrance door she had watched a maid use earlier in the day.

The lock shut behind her, and a sharp sound echoed in the night's stillness. The hinges creaked in protest as she pushed the heavy door open. A chill creeping in made her shiver involuntarily. She pulled her thin coat tighter around her shoulders, the fabric barely offering warmth against the biting cold. Her once-sturdy boots, now scuffed and worn, crunched against the cobblestone streets, while the scratchy wool stockings beneath her faded dress did little to fend off the brisk wind.

But a sense of urgency fueled her; she didn't care about her discomfort. Hurrying down the dimly lit streets, she expertly navigated between the clattering carriages, each casting flickering shadows in the gaslight. The murmurs of passersby trailed behind her, a cacophony of curiosity and judgment that she chose to ignore. The city loomed large, its towering buildings standing like sentinels, and the streets stretched out endlessly before her, an intricate maze that both fascinated and intimidated her. Every corner she turned seemed to reveal another stretch of the urban landscape, filled with the promise of anonymity and adventure.

Lily rounded the corner of the bustling street a bit too quickly, her heart racing with the thrill of her hurried pace. Suddenly, she collided with a young man who had been casually walking in the opposite direction. He appeared to be no more than nineteen or twenty, with tousled dark hair that caught the late afternoon sun. His warm brown eyes widened in surprise as they flicked down to meet hers, momentarily reflecting the soft glow of the golden light around them. The air was thick with the scent of freshly baked goods from a nearby café, but in that instant, she could only focus on the startled look on the stranger's face.

"Whoa—where are you off to in such a hurry?"

Lily stepped back, wiping her nose. "I have to find my sister."

The young man frowned. "Alone? Where is she?"

Lily hesitated. "She's... she's waiting for me."

He studied her for a long moment. "You're far too little to be wandering Boston alone."

"I am not little!" she snapped, her lip trembling.

His expression softened. "Okay, okay. What's your sister's name?"

Lily straightened her coat. "Katie."

The young man's brow furrowed. "Katie... Taylor?"

Lily froze.

His voice dropped. "I think I know where she is."

Lily's pulse pounded in her ears. "You do?"

A strange look passed over his face, unreadable. "Come on," he said, offering his hand. "I'll take you to her."

She hesitated, her heart pounding in her chest as uncertainty washed over her—but deep down, she knew she had no other choice. The dim light of the fading day cast a warm glow around them, illuminating the worry etched on her face. As she looked into his eyes, searching for reassurance, she felt the moment's weight press heavily upon her. With a deep breath and quiet resolve, she finally reached out, taking his hand, feeling the warmth of his grasp enveloping hers like a lifeline.

Chapter Thirty-Five: The Vanishing

The sound of hurried footsteps echoed against the polished wooden floors of the sprawling Taylor estate, each thud a stark reminder of the tension in the air. Nathaniel Taylor paced restlessly near the tall front windows, which framed a foreboding view of the darkening sky outside. His jaw was clenched tight, the muscles tense with worry, while his hands, balled into fists, betrayed his inner turmoil. The rich, dark oak of the furniture around him seemed to absorb the anxiety that pulsed through the room, and the faint scent of polished wood mingled with the mustiness of forgotten corners in the grand old house.

"Katherine," his voice was sharp yet filled with concern. "Lily is missing."

Sitting by the fireplace, Katherine looked up, her body tensing at his words.

"What do you mean missing?" she demanded, standing abruptly.

Nathaniel exhaled, trying to keep his emotions in check. "Officer Dean received word from Rosehill Orphanage this morning. Lily is gone. "Katherine's heart dropped to her stomach.

No.

She shook her head as if she could shake away the

reality of his words. "That's not possible. She wouldn't just run away. She—she knows I've been looking for her!"

"I know," Nathaniel said gravely, "which is why this doesn't make sense." Katherine staggered back a step, her mind racing.

Her sister.

Her sweet, innocent Lily.

"Someone took her," she whispered, her voice barely audible.

Nathaniel's eyes darkened. "That's what I fear."

Officer Dean and Captain Calloway stood outside Eleanor Ward's office, waiting for answers.

The matron looked deeply shaken, wringing her hands together as she tried to recall every detail. "I—I swear, I don't know how it happened," she insisted. "Lily was fine just last night. She went to bed as usual. This morning, she was gone."

Officer Dean folded his arms. "Did she say anything unusual before she disappeared? Did she mention anyone?"

Eleanor hesitated, thinking back. "Well... she did talk about Katie. That's all she ever talked about."

Katherine. Nathaniel, standing in the doorway, felt his stomach sink.

"She was looking for me," Katherine murmured.

Officer Dean turned back to Eleanor. "Was there anything left behind? Any notes? Clues?"

Eleanor nodded quickly and rushed to her desk. She pulled out a piece of crumpled parchment smeared with ink and childlike handwriting.

Dean took it, reading aloud.

"Katie, I'll find you. Wait for me."

Katherine pressed her hand to her mouth, fighting

back tears.

Officer Dean set the paper down, his expression grim. "She left on her own."

"But she didn't make it to me," Katherine whispered.

Nathaniel exchanged a sharp look with Officer Dean.

"So, the question is," Nathaniel said darkly, "who found her first?"

By nightfall, Captain Calloway sent officers into the streets to question anyone who might have seen a small blonde girl wandering alone. It wasn't until a baker's assistant mentioned a little girl speaking to a young man that the puzzle began to take shape. Officer Dean tracked down the description. Tall. Dark hair. Serious demeanor. Someone who looked like he didn't belong in the city. Then, finally, a name. Owen Walters. The name sent a chill through Nathaniel and Katherine alike. Dean looked up from his notes. "That name mean anything to you?" Katherine felt the blood drain from her face.

"He works at Ridgefield," she whispered.

A heavy silence filled the room.

Nathaniel cursed under his breath.

Dean stood abruptly. "Then we know where she is."

Ridgefield Asylum. Lily sat curled on a cot in a dimly lit room. The air smelled of antiseptic and something musty and old. She shivered, her small fingers gripping the blanket wrapped around her shoulders. She didn't understand. Where was Katie? The last thing she remembered was the man with dark eyes leading her down a long road, his grip firm but not cruel. He had told her he knew where Katie was. But this wasn't Katie's home. This place felt wrong. The heavy door creaked open, and Lily's breath caught as a man entered. Tall. Pale.

Cold blue eyes that held no warmth. Dr. Julian Aldridge. He didn't smile. He merely studied her, as if she were a specimen under glass.

"You look just like your sister," he mused, stepping closer. Lily shrank away.

"Where's Katie?" she asked, her voice trembling.

Aldridge tilted his head slightly.

"Oh, my dear child." His voice was smooth, almost soft. "She's coming for you."

Lily's eyes widened.

"Then let me go to her!"

Aldridge's smile was slow, calculated.

"Not yet," he murmured. "First, I need to send her an invitation."

He turned to the nurse beside him.

"Bring me my writing materials. It's time for Miss Taylor to come home."

Katherine gripped the table's edge in the Taylor Estate, her entire body trembling.

"She's there," she whispered. "She's at Ridgefield."

Nathaniel rubbed a hand over his face. "We'll get her out."

But Katherine was already moving.

"No. I have to go."

Nathaniel's head snapped up. "Absolutely not."

Katherine turned on him, her blue eyes blazing. "I am not waiting. I will not let Aldridge use her against me!"

Daniel stepped forward, placing a firm but gentle hand on her arm.

"We're not letting you walk into that hell alone."

Katherine looked at him, at the man who had stood by her side and risked everything for her. This wasn't just about love. This was about trust. She gave a sharp nod.

"Then we plan. But we do not wait."

Daniel's grip tightened. "Agreed."

Nathaniel sighed. He had never seen Katherine this determined.

For the first time, she wasn't asking for permission. She was taking control. And this time—she would not lose.

Chapter Thirty-Six: The Trap is Set

March 1856

At the Taylor Estate, the sun began to set over Boston, casting long, gold-streaked shadows across the study's polished wood floors. Nathaniel Taylor stood near the window, arms crossed, his sharp brown eyes narrowed at the sight of a lone courier approaching the estate. He was dressed in a gray coat with a matching hat pulled low over his forehead and moved with purposeful precision as he strode up the steps. He did not knock. Instead, he reached into his coat, pulled out a pristine white envelope, and placed it directly into the waiting hands of a footman. Without a word, he turned and disappeared into the misty evening air. Nathaniel was already moving before the footman could react. He snatched the envelope, his pulse pounding with unease as he read the name written in sharp, slanted ink.

Miss Katherine Ann Taylor

His grip tightened and without hesitation, he broke the seal and unfolded the letter inside, his stomach twisting with dread as he read its contents. Behind him, the study doors creaked open. Katherine stepped inside, her blue eyes scanning his face with instant alarm.

"What is it?" she asked, voice sharp with suspicion.

Nathaniel hesitated, his heart racing as he extended the weathered envelope toward her. The flickering candlelight cast shadows on the surface, illuminating the fine creases of the parchment. With a gentle, trembling hand, she accepted the letter, her fingers brushing against the cool paper. As she unfolded it, the faint scent of aged ink mingled with the air, and she took a deep breath to steady herself before reading the carefully composed words.

My Dearest Katherine Taylor,

I hope you are well.

You left Ridgefield rather abruptly, but I have not forgotten you. I regret the circumstances that forced us apart—I truly believed we were making progress.

You will be pleased to know I have welcomed a new guest into our care: a lost and frightened child searching for her beloved sister. Sweet Lily is in excellent hands. She is calling for you at night, though I have assured her you are safe and will come for her soon. I do hope you come, Miss Taylor. I would hate for her to suffer the same fate as you. Ridgefield is always open to its most treasured patients. Do not keep me waiting.

Warmest regards,

Dr. Julian Aldridge

The room blurred around her. Katherine could barely breathe as her hands clutched the letter, her nails digging into the parchment's edges: her sister, Lily.

"She's there," she choked out, barely above a whisper.

Nathaniel's expression hardened his lips, a thin line of fury. "We'll get her out."

But Katherine was already shaking her head.

"No. I'll get her out."

Nathaniel stepped forward. "Katherine, listen to

me. You are not walking back into that nightmare—"

"I won't leave Lily in there!" she snapped, her voice raw, edged with desperation.

Nathaniel exhaled slowly, trying to keep his temper in check.

"I understand that," he said carefully, his tone dark and controlled. "But if you go alone, you won't leave."

Katherine's breath trembled as she prepared herself for the challenge ahead, her heart pounding in her chest. She squared her shoulders, determination flickering in her eyes. She would not allow herself to lose her sister; not now, not ever. Just then, a warm and reassuring hand enveloped her arm, grounding her amid the turmoil. She turned to find Daniel standing beside her, his dark eyes reflecting a steadfast calmness. The intensity of his gaze felt both protective and unwavering, providing her with the strength she needed to face the uncertain path before them.

"If you go," he said, voice low, "then I go too."

Nathaniel still did not like it. His niece was stubborn to a fault, just like her mother had been, and he knew no amount of reasoning would keep her from this.

"Fine," he bit out at last. "But we will do this the smart way."

Martha, hovering by the door, wrung her hands before stepping forward.

"I—I can help," she offered hesitantly.

Katherine turned toward her, eyes wild with urgency. "How?"

Martha swallowed. "I—I've seen how women come and go from Ridgefield. How they speak to the nurses, how they're examined, how they're processed. If you must go back in, I can at least tell you what to expect."

Katherine nodded, gripping Martha's hands. "Thank you."

"We're working on a legal removal," Nathaniel said, "but Aldridge will stall. That means we don't have time to wait for the law."

Katherine lifted her chin. "Then I won't wait."

Elias had never intended to eavesdrop, yet he found himself frozen in place when he overheard the mention of Aldridge's name, tinged with Katherine's desperation, alongside the enigmatic word "Ridgefield." He had been standing outside, leaning against the cold, unforgiving stone of the Taylor estate, the chill creeping through his jacket as he wrestled with the decision of whether to knock on the door or simply walk away. He had come to apologize, to confess that he genuinely wanted Katherine to be happy—even if that happiness meant she would be with Daniel.

But upon hearing her name intertwined with Daniel's, a tight, painful twist coiled in his chest, squeezing the breath from his lungs. His mind raced as he grasped the implications: she was planning to return to him. A surge of adrenaline coursed through Elias as he stepped back from the entrance, his heart pounding like a war drum. Daniel was a man who thrived on chaos and control, and now he was leading her dangerously close to the edge.

Without a second thought, Elias turned sharply on his heel, a reckless plan already forming in his mind. He had to reach Ridgefield first. The name echoed in his head like a siren's call, a place shrouded in secrets and peril, but he couldn't allow Katherine to face it alone. She deserved better than to be ensnared in Daniel's web, and he was determined to rescue her, no matter the cost.

The air inside Ridgefield felt thick and stale, suffocating in a way that tightened Lily's small chest with each labored breath. She sat curled on the narrow cot, her knees drawn up tightly to her chin, with her arms wrapped protectively around them. The blanket she clutched bore the unmistakable scent of antiseptic mingled with something musty, suggesting it hadn't been washed in years, a reminder of the sterile yet oppressive environment that surrounded her. Across the dimly lit room, where the flickering fluorescent bulb cast erratic shadows, Dr. Aldridge sat in his worn leather chair, his gaze fixed intently upon her. The intensity of his watchfulness sent a shiver down her spine. He wasn't like her father. He didn't shout in rage or hurl objects across the room, yet there was a chilling calmness about him that felt equally threatening. For what seemed like an eternity, neither of them spoke, the silence only broken by the rhythmic ticking of the clock on his cluttered desk, each tick echoing in the stillness like an ominous countdown.

"Why do you want to hurt Katie?"

Aldridge stilled. For the first time since she had arrived, he looked surprised.

"I don't want to hurt her," he said slowly as if the very idea was foreign to him.

Lily's little brows furrowed. "But you look angry."

Aldridge exhaled through his nose, leaning back in his chair. "I want to help her," he corrected.

Lily's hands curled into fists around the fabric of her dress. "No, you don't."

Aldridge tilted his head slightly, his cold blue eyes sharp. Curious. Studying.

"You're very certain of that," he mused.

For a long moment, he said nothing. Then, his fingers tapped against the wooden armrest of his chair.

"That's where you're wrong," he murmured.

Lily's heart pounded but she didn't back down.

"Why do you want to hurt her?" she asked again, more firmly this time.

Aldridge let out a soft, breathless laugh that hung in the air like a fragile whisper, void of any genuine mirth. The sound echoed off the dimly lit walls, unsettling in its haunting quality. He stood slowly, each movement deliberate, as his dark, tailored coat shifted around him, the fabric whispering against itself. Stepping closer, the faint scent of tobacco and leather enveloped him, mingling with the mustiness of the room, creating an atmosphere thick with unspoken tension.

"I don't expect you to understand," he said. His voice was eerily calm, almost gentle. "You see her as she wants to be seen. The devoted sister. The golden daughter."

Lily gritted her teeth. "She is good."

Aldridge smiled—but it wasn't a kind smile.

"She is a lie, little one," he murmured. "Just like I was."

Lily's small hands tightened into fists. "You're lying."

Aldridge kneeled in front of her, his voice dropping to a whisper.

"She left you once already, didn't she?"

Lily's breath hitched.

"She didn't leave me," she whispered.

Aldridge's smile widened, but his eyes were unreadable.

"She will," he said softly.

Lily's entire body felt cold. She stared at him,

uncertainty flickering in her young, blue eyes. That was when Aldridge knew he had planted the seed. He straightened, smoothing the creases from his coat.

"She'll come for you," he said. "She'll step right back into Ridgefield. And when she does…"

He smiled again.

"She will never leave."

Lily pressed her teeth into her trembling lip, fighting against the cascade of tears that threatened to spill from her shimmering silver-blue eyes. The air in the dimly lit room felt stifling, thick with unspoken words and the weight of regret as she watched Aldridge. His tall, broad frame was silhouetted against the doorway, each deliberate step he took resonating like a tolling bell, amplifying the heaviness in her chest. Just before he disappeared into the corridor, a flicker of resolve ignited within her, illuminating her mind amidst the murky emotions. "Wait," she called out, her voice fragile yet piercing, breaking through the suffocating silence that enveloped them both.

"Katie's not a liar."

Aldridge paused. He didn't turn back around.

"I think you're the one who's scared," Lily said softly. "Scared of her."

A heavy silence enveloped the dimly lit room, thick enough that one could almost hear the faint tick of a distant clock. Suddenly, a quiet, breathless chuckle broke through the tension, reverberating off the stark white walls. Moments later, Dr. Aldridge emerged from the shadows, his weary eyes glimmering with a mix of amusement and contemplation. He paused briefly, glancing back at the closed door, before softly clicking the lock into place, sealing away whatever secrets lay behind him.

Chapter Thirty-Seven: Into the Lion's Den
March 6, 1856 – The Taylor Estate

The fire crackled softly in the grand hearth of the Taylor estate's study, sending flickering shadows dancing across the polished mahogany walls adorned with rich, dark leather-bound books. The warmth radiated from the flames, yet it did little to alleviate the palpable tension that hung in the air, heavy like a thick fog. The delicate scent of aged wood mingled with the faint aroma of burning pine, but these sensory comforts did nothing to quell the unspoken fears that gnawed at the edges of their minds. In one corner, an ornate chandelier cast a dim glow, its crystals refracting light in a way that felt almost mocking against the gravity of the situation. Each person in the room wore a mask of unyielding determination, their expressions resolute yet betraying glimmers of anxiety. The silence stretched like an elastic band, ready to snap at the slightest provocation, as a sense of finality loomed over them, binding them together in this tense moment of uncertainty and resolve.

Nathaniel stood with his hands firmly clasped behind his back, his expression a blend of stern resolve and quiet contemplation. The flickering candlelight danced around the room, casting long, deep shadows beneath his piercing blue eyes, which held a hint of unspoken thoughts. Across from him, Katherine sat stiffly on the plush velvet settee, the rich burgundy fabric contrasting sharply with the pale hue of her dress. She maintained a rigid posture, her back perfectly straight, while her delicate fingers were intertwined in her lap, betraying a hint of tension. The air between them crackled with unspoken words, heavy with anticipation and the weight of their shared history.

Daniel leaned forward, his elbows braced on his knees, jaw tight. His usually composed demeanor was slipping, frustration peeking through the cracks.

Nathaniel exhaled sharply and ran a hand through his hair. "We're running out of time," he muttered, his voice low and clipped. He turned to Katherine. "If we do this, there is no turning back. Are you sure?"

Katherine's heart pounded, but her voice remained steady. "Lily is waiting for me."

Nathaniel held her gaze for a long moment before giving a small, reluctant nod. "

Elias stood before the imposing iron gates of Ridgefield, a shiver racing down his spine as the damp, thick fog enveloped him like a shroud. The chill in the air seemed to seep through his clothes, and his pulse raced beneath his ribs, a frantic drumbeat of urgency. He had no formal plan, only a visceral, desperate need to breach the fortress-like entrance that loomed before him.

As he took a deep breath, he caught sight of a heavyset guard who emerged from the shadows, a flickering lantern in hand casting a faint glow that barely penetrated the murky air. The guard's brow furrowed as he squinted at Elias, his broad shoulders creating an imposing figure against the darkness. "State your business," he barked, his voice gruff and unwavering, demanding a justification for Elias's presence in this foreboding place.

Elias cleared his throat, forcing an air of calm. "I've come to see my cousin, Mary."

The guard narrowed his gaze. "We don't take visitors unannounced."

Elias feigned exasperation. "I was told she'd be available for visitors today."

The guard muttered something under his breath before turning and waving him through. "Wait in the visitor's parlor."

As Elias pushed open the massive wooden doors, a wave of sensations enveloped him. The air was thick with the pungent aroma of medicinal herbs, their earthy scent mingling with the cool, damp fragrance of stone. A metallic undertone, reminiscent of copper and blood, clung to the atmosphere, sharp and unsettling, invoking an instinctive sense of caution as he stepped into the dimly lit space beyond.

A nurse led him into a small, dimly lit waiting room. As he sat, he overheard two nurses whispering.

"...the new child. Dr. Aldridge's special case."

"...She won't stop asking for her sister."

Elias's stomach churned violently, a tumultuous knot of anxiety twisting within him. Lily. The mere mention of her name sent a wave of tension coursing through his body. He clenched his hands into tight fists, his knuckles whitening as he fought to regain control. With each deep breath, he attempted to steady the rapid thrum of his heartbeat, but the weight of uncertainty pressed heavily on his chest, leaving him grappling with a rush of conflicting emotions.

When Dean arrived at Ridgefield, he was led down a narrow, poorly lit corridor, the flickering fluorescent lights casting eerie shadows along the faded, peeling walls. The air was heavy with the scent of antiseptic and something else—something stale. At the end of the corridor, he was stopped in front of a cluttered office door, the chipped paint barely hanging on. Inside, a broad-shouldered man with cold gray eyes sat behind an imposing oak desk, its surface littered with stacks of papers, empty coffee cups, and an assortment of pens that seemed to have long lost their ink.

Mr. Grayson, the Head Orderly, exuded an air of authority that was both intimidating and unsettling. Dressed in a wrinkled white shirt and dark slacks, he appeared unbothered by the chaos surrounding him. He didn't look up immediately, his gaze locked on a thick ledger, the pages filled with meticulously handwritten entries. His fingers moved with a slow, methodical rhythm, tapping against the page like a metronome as he flipped through the entries, seemingly oblivious to Dean's presence. The dim light caught the sharp angles of his face, highlighting the sternness in his expression and giving him an almost predatory demeanor.

"You're here for the position?"

"Yes, sir."

Grayson's gaze flicked up, sharp and assessing. "Experience?"

"I've handled difficult individuals before," Dean answered carefully.

Grayson smirked. "Difficult individuals, huh? You mean the ones who claw and scream, or the ones who weep and beg?"

Dean forced his expression to remain neutral.

Grayson leaned forward, his voice dropping to a conspiratorial tone. "You understand, of course, that Ridgefield has rules."

Dean nodded.

Grayson smirked. "Good. Here's rule number one: The patients lie. Always." He flipped another page in the ledger. "Rule number two: You follow orders without question."

Dean's jaw tightened.

"And rule number three," Grayson continued, his voice lowering, "you don't hesitate to use force when necessary."

Dean met his gaze evenly. "Understood."

Grayson studied him for a long moment before giving a slow nod. "We'll see if you last."

The hired carriage lurched to a jarring stop outside Ridgefield's imposing iron gates, their twisted vines and rusted bars casting eerie shadows in the waning light. Katherine's fingers clenched the fabric of her skirts, the coarse material grounding her amidst the storm of anxiety swirling within her. Her heart hammered wildly against her ribcage, each thud echoing the apprehension that threatened to swallow her whole. Beside her, Daniel sat rigid, his jaw set like granite, the tension in his shoulders betraying his calm demeanor. His grip on her hand was firm yet reassuring, a steady anchor in the face of uncertainty. The faint scent of damp earth and approaching rain mixed with the lingering aroma of leather from the carriage, filling the air with a heavy tension as they prepared to confront whatever lay beyond those foreboding gates.

"Are you ready?" he asked, his voice low.

Katherine inhaled sharply. "I have to be."

The iron gates groaned open, and the two stepped out.

A guard stepped forward, scrutinizing them. "State your business."

Daniel straightened. "My wife wishes to return to Ridgefield. She believes this is where she belongs."

The guard's brows lifted in surprise. His gaze shifted to Katherine. "That true?"

Katherine forced herself to smile.

"It's Katie now," she said softly, tilting her head, mirroring Aldridge's condescending tone. "And yes, I miss being here."

The guard hesitated, then stepped aside. "Welcome back, Mrs. Hahn."

Her stomach twisted with anxiety as she stepped through the heavy doors, the metallic clang echoing in the dimly lit hallway. The air inside was thick with unsettling memories—the faint echoes of patients' cries, the sterile chilling presence of cold stone walls, and the lingering scent of lye mingling with an undercurrent of palpable fear. Each step she took seemed to revive the ghosts of her past, shadows flickering at the edges of her mind.

At the end of the corridor stood Dr. Aldridge, a formidable figure draped in a pristine white coat. He exuded an air of authority, his stance reminiscent of a king surveying his court. His lips curled into a slow, deliberate smirk that hinted at both amusement and disdain, creating an unsettling contrast against the seriousness of his environment. The flickering fluorescent lights above cast a harsh glow on his features, accentuating the sharp angles of his face and the cold calculation in his eyes.

"Katie," he murmured.

Katherine's skin crawled, but she smiled.

"Dr. Aldridge," she said smoothly.

His brown eyes narrowed slightly.

"Katie," he repeated as if testing the weight of the name.

Daniel sighed heavily. "She's been struggling since leaving," he said. "She feels Ridgefield is where she belongs."

Aldridge's gaze drifted to Katherine, studying her.

"Do you?" he asked.

Katherine smiled just enough. "I do."

Aldridge held her gaze for a long moment before nodding.

"Then let's get you settled, shall we?"

Chapter Thirty-Eight: Fractured Truths

The air in Dr. Julian Aldridge's office was thick with stale heaviness, tinged with the unmistakable aroma of ink and parchment that whispered of countless hours spent in scholarly pursuits. A faint, medicinal scent hung in the air like a ghost, creeping around the edges of Katherine's senses, both unsettling and oddly comforting. She sat with impeccable poise, her hands delicately folded in her lap, the epitome of graceful composure as she met the gaze of the man before her. Observing her intently, Dr. Aldridge scrutinized her like a rare specimen under glass, his fingers steepled thoughtfully beneath his chin, elbows resting on the polished surface of the desk. The tension in the room was palpable, a silent exchange of curiosity and contemplation swirling around them.

"You've come back willingly," he murmured, his voice quiet, deliberate. "That is quite the change of heart, Katie."

Katherine forced herself to remain impassive at the name. She had expected this. She had prepared for this.

"I needed to," she answered softly, keeping her voice even. "The world outside—it wasn't what I thought it would be. I didn't belong."

Aldridge leaned forward slightly. "And what makes

you believe you belong here?"

Katherine allowed her gaze to wander across the room, taking in the soft, dim lighting that bathed the space in a muted glow, and the pristine sterility of the surroundings that seemed to whisper promises of calm and order. Every surface gleamed with a clinical precision, designed to evoke a sense of peace and healing. Yet, beneath this veneer of tranquility, the walls closed in around her like a heavy blanket, smothering her with a sense of confinement and unrest.

"I feel real here," she said finally, her tone measured but distant. "Outside, it felt like I was watching myself live someone else's life."

Aldridge hummed thoughtfully. He was watching her carefully, weighing every word.

"Fascinating," he murmured. "Most would say the opposite. That confinement makes them feel less real."

Katherine hesitated just long enough to make him believe her uncertainty was genuine. "Perhaps that is true... for some."

His lips twitched at the corners, something resembling satisfaction flickering across his face.

Aldridge stood, moving toward a shelf lined with medical texts. His fingers trailed along the spines of the books, stopping at a particularly aged volume.

"We'll start fresh, then," he declared, turning back to her. "I will oversee your treatment personally."

Katherine kept her face neutral, but her mind was already spinning. *Perfect. If he's focused on me, he won't see the others coming.*

Daniel's fists clenched tightly, his nails biting into his palms, drawing faint crimson lines against his skin as he sat in the stark, sterile waiting area. The seconds stretched into an eternity, each tick of the clock a relentless reminder of his growing anxiety. Something was dreadfully wrong. It had been far too long since they had taken Katherine away, and now he was left in this desolate space, feeling utterly powerless. His stomach twisted and churned at the thought of her alone and vulnerable. *I should have never let her do this*, the guilt gnawed at him like a persistent shadow, darkening his thoughts.

A guard passed, and Daniel shot to his feet. "How long will she be in evaluation?"

The man barely spared him a glance. "As long as Dr. Aldridge deems necessary."

Daniel's jaw tightened painfully, a muscle twitching beneath the strain of his emotions. He yearned to demand answers, to burst through the chaos and fight his way to her side, but he forced himself to remain still, every fiber of his being resisting the urge to act. This was a delicate game, and he had to play his part perfectly. *If I push too hard, I'll ruin everything* he thought, the weight of those words pressing down on him like a looming storm.

Yet, amid the tension, a chilling realization sliced through him with the sharpness of a blade: *I love her.* The truth struck him with a fierce intensity, igniting a deep fear within—the kind that curled around his heart like a vise. The thought of losing her now filled him with dread so profound that he felt as if the ground beneath him might give way. *If I lose her, I won't survive it.* The sobering acknowledgment settled heavily in his chest, intertwining hope and despair in a volatile dance, and he stood there, caught between the agony of his desire and the necessity of restraint.

Elias glided silently through the echoing halls of Ridgefield, making a conscious effort to maintain an air of casual confidence as if he truly belonged in this sterile environment. He had adopted a false identity—Mary Montgomery, a fictitious cousin—and, to his relief, no one had raised an eyebrow. Then, like a moth drawn to a flame, he spotted her.

A small figure meandered alongside a nurse, her golden curls shimmering like sunlight in the faint hospital lighting. Her delicate frame moved with an unmistakable hesitance, each step a whisper of uncertainty. Elias felt his breath hitch in his throat.

Lily.

His heart pounded violently against his ribs, and every fiber of his being went tense with emotion. He was on the verge of calling out to her, of rushing forward to bridge the distance that had grown between them, but a deep instinct cautioned him—not yet. Instead, he trailed silently behind her, his pulse a relentless drum in his ears. I've found her. Now, I have to devise a plan to get her out.

Cassandra Jones sat restrained to a chair, her wrists bound to the arms. Her breath came in shallow pants, her entire body trembling. The room was sterile and cold, the dim oil lamps casting eerie shadows along the walls. Dean stood beside her, his stomach tight with unease.

"She refuses to cooperate," the head nurse stated. "She must be reminded of the rules."

Dean leaned in, lowering his voice to a whisper.

"You have to trust me."

Cassandra flinched. "No one can be trusted here."

Dean's eyes softened. "I'm not like them. But you have to do what they say. For now."

Cassandra studied his face intently, a flicker of

fear crossing her features, battling against a burgeoning sense of hope. With a subtle, almost imperceptible nod, she affirmed her feelings. At that moment, Dean straightened, a renewed sense of purpose washing over him, just as the head nurse cast a sly smirk, her eyes glinting with a mix of amusement and knowing.

"See? They always break."

Dean clenched his jaw, swallowing back his fury. No, she isn't broken. Not yet. And I won't let her be.

Within the dim confines of the Taylor Estate, Martha fervently repeated her prayers, the words spilling from her lips with an urgency that matched the unease clawing at her insides. An ominous feeling settled over her, as if a storm was gathering force just beyond the ancient walls. The heavy silence wrapped around her, thick and suffocating, amplifying the sense that something inevitable was drawing near.

Suddenly, the front door creaked open, the sound grating against the stillness like a warning bell. Martha's heart stuttered in her chest, her breath hitching as she froze in place. A shadow elongated across the polished timber floor, stretching like dark fingers reaching into the light. She turned slowly, the rag she had been clutching slipping from her grasp and falling unnoticed to the ground.

There, framed in the doorway, stood Margaret. The sight of her struck a chord of dread in Martha's soul. Pale and gaunt, Margaret looked almost spectral, her eyes wide and haunted, as though she had slipped through the veil of reality. For a long, breathless moment, the two women exchanged a heavy silence, the air thickening with unspoken fears. Finally, Margaret's voice broke through the stillness—hoarse, quiet, and laden with a weight that seemed to echo with the promise of something dark to come.

"Where is everyone?"

Margaret moved through the house as if walking through a graveyard. Everything felt wrong. The silence pressed against her, thick and unnatural.

Martha swallowed hard. "Margaret…"

Margaret turned, her face unreadable.

"Tell me the truth."

Martha hesitated. Margaret's expression darkened. "Where is Katherine?"

Martha exhaled shakily. "She's… she's gone."

Margaret stiffened. "Gone?"

Martha's voice cracked. "She went back. For Lily."

Margaret swayed uncertainly, her hand grasping the cool, polished banister for support. Katherine had come back to Ridgefield, the familiar surroundings now feeling alien and oppressive. A shaky exhale escaped her lips, filled with a mix of anxiety and relief. She had escaped a suffocating nightmare, only to find herself confronted by something even more daunting, lurking in the shadows of her return.

Chapter Thirty-Nine: A Grave Conversation

The earth was still fresh, and the simple wooden marker stood stark against the morning light. The wind carried the scent of damp soil, the remains of an unsettled winter lingering in the air. Margaret stood before the grave, arms crossed, her shawl wrapped tightly around her shoulders as if it could shield her from the cold—or the memories. She stared down at the mound of dirt, her expression unreadable.

"You always thought you were untouchable, didn't you?" she murmured.

The wind whispered through the trees, silent between her and the grave.

"You were a terrible husband." Her voice was quiet, but the words were sharp, cutting through the stillness. "A terrible father."

Her hands curled into fists, her knuckles white. "You never loved me. Not really. You saw me as something to possess, to control. And I was too young and foolish to understand what I was walking into when I married you."

She exhaled sharply, shaking her head. "I should have fought harder. I should have chosen Nathaniel. I loved him, Reginald. Not you. Never you."

Margaret let out a bitter laugh, the sound hollow. "And now he's back. My Nathaniel." She swallowed hard, voice softening. "Do I still have a chance? After all this time?"

She closed her eyes, inhaling deeply. "I don't know. But I know this—I will get my daughters out of Ridgefield. And after that... after that, I will finally be free of you."

She turned on her heel and walked away, leaving Reginald to the silence of his unmarked grave.

Margaret stepped inside the warmth of the house, starkly contrasting to the chill outside. She found Martha in the sitting room, the older woman wringing her hands, her face lined with worry.

Martha looked up as Margaret entered. "Did it help?"

Margaret hesitated. "No."

Martha nodded solemnly. "I didn't think it would."

Margaret sat beside her, her voice steadier now. "Tell me everything."

Martha took a deep breath. "The plan is in motion, but it won't be easy. Ridgefield is watching Katherine closely. And Lily... she's being kept under special care. We have people on the inside, but Aldridge is unpredictable."

Margaret's expression darkened. "I don't care how difficult it is. I will do whatever it takes."

Martha studied her for a long moment before nodding. "I believe you." Then, softer, "And after? What happens when your girls are safe?"

Margaret hesitated, her gaze distant. "Then, I go after Nathaniel."

Martha's lips pressed into a thin line. "You never stopped loving him."

Margaret smiled, small but real. "No. I never did."

At the Ridgeland Asylum, the ceiling was cracked, a thin line stretching across the plaster like a fracture waiting to split. Katherine stared at it, unmoving.

She had played the part of the obedient patient well—too well—but she was not broken. *I survived this place once. I will survive it again.* She had learned from Mary-Alice, Ellie, and her own suffering. Katherine sat up slowly, listening to the quiet hum of the asylum, the shuffling of footsteps outside her door, and the occasional cry from a distant room. She had been watching, studying, and waiting for the moment to strike. Her mind drifted to Lily. She was here, somewhere, and Katherine would find her. She had to.

Elias paced in a dimly lit supply room, his hands clenched at his sides. "We don't have time."

Dean leaned against the shelves, his jaw tight. "If we rush it, we'll get caught."

"We'll lose them if we wait too long," Elias snapped.

Dean exhaled sharply. "I know."

They had worked carefully, quietly. But time was slipping away, and Aldridge grew more suspicious by the day.

Dean rubbed his forehead. "Aldridge is planning something. I overheard one of the nurses—he will test Katherine's compliance soon."

Elias's stomach turned. "What does that mean?"

Dean's expression darkened. "I don't know. But we need to move soon. Very soon."

Julian Aldridge watched from his office window as Katherine moved through the halls. Something was wrong. She had been too cooperative, too docile, and she was hiding something. His mother had done the same. She had smiled when she was supposed to. She had played the wife and mother role until she hadn't. Aldridge's fingers tapped against the desk. *She needs a test.*

He turned to his head nurse. "Prepare the treatment

room."

The nurse hesitated. "For...?"

Aldridge's gaze was steady. "For Katherine Taylor."

Nathaniel sat stiffly in the captain's office, his fingers pressed against his temple.

"There has to be a way," he said.

Captain Calloway sighed. "The problem is, the law protects Ridgefield. Questionable, but legal nonetheless."

Nathaniel's jaw tightened. "And Lily?"

"She's a minor. And her mother is missing. That complicates things."

Nathaniel exhaled sharply. "So, what do we do?"

The captain leaned forward. "There is a way. But it will take time. And I don't think your niece has that luxury."

Nathaniel realized then that legal action wouldn't be enough. He would have to act outside the law if he wanted to save Katherine and Lily.

Chapter Forty: The Breaking Point

The treatment room was eerily quiet, except for the humming of the electrical machine. Katherine lay strapped to the cold metal table, her pulse hammering against her skin. Dr. Julian Aldridge stood over her, his expression unreadable as he traced the leather straps across her wrists, ensuring they were tight. He moved methodically, each motion calculated and precise—as if she were nothing more than an experiment.

"We need to test your progress, Katherine," he said, adjusting the knobs on the machine. "You've been so obedient. Let's see if that holds under… pressure."

A nurse stepped forward and secured the electrodes against Katherine's temples. The coolness of the metal sent a shiver through her. Her heart pounded. She knew what was coming. Pain. Darkness. Losing herself again. But this time, something inside her refused to break.

Daniel had been waiting, listening, drowning in helplessness. His fists clenched at his sides. Something was happening to Katherine.

Elias sat beside him, tense. "We need to think this through—"

Daniel snapped. "If I wait any longer, she could die in there."

Without hesitation, he stormed through the asylum

halls, pushing past staff.

An orderly moved to stop him. Daniel didn't hesitate—his fist connected with the man's jaw, sending him sprawling. Every part of him burned with one thought—he would not let them hurt her again.

Katherine clenched her fists as the machine buzzed to life. The sharp scent of burning dust filled the air. Then—BANG. The door slammed open so violently it nearly cracked the frame. A figure stormed inside. Daniel. His gun was drawn, his breathing sharp and furious. The room erupted into chaos. Orderlies rushed him—he swung wildly, knocking one back into a tray of instruments, sending metal clattering to the floor.

Aldridge stepped back, his face composed but his eyes dark. "You have no authority here, Mr. Hahn."

Daniel aimed the gun directly at him. "I have more than you think."

An orderly lunged—Daniel fired. The gunshot ripped through the air, and one of the orderlies collapsed, groaning. Katherine gasped. Daniel. For the first time in weeks, she felt a flicker of hope.

Elias and Officer Dean rushed in moments later, and weapons were drawn. Daniel made it to Katherine first, his hands moving quickly to undo the straps. Her wrists were raw, her body trembling, but she was awake. Alive.

"You found me," she whispered.

Daniel's breath was unsteady as he cupped her face gently.

"I'll always find you."

Officer Dean turned to Aldridge, his voice cold.

"By order of the Boston Board of Health, Ridgefield Asylum is under investigation. You are no longer in control here."

Aldridge merely smirked. "Investigate all you like, Officer. My work is important."

Dean's jaw clenched. "Your work is cruelty. And it ends today."

Elias and Daniel moved quickly, getting Katherine out of the treatment room. In a nearby chamber, they found Mary-Alice, bruised but alive. Katherine ran to her, clutching her nurse's hands.

"I thought I lost you," Katherine whispered.

Mary-Alice stroked her hair, voice shaking. "You never will."

Meanwhile, Elias carried Cassandra from another ward—her body was weak, but her spirit was fighting.

"You're safe now," Daniel reassured them.

But the battle wasn't over yet.

The heavy asylum doors creaked ominously as they swung open, revealing a dimly lit hallway filled with the faint scent of antiseptic and despair. A group of officials, clad in dark, formal attire, stormed inside with a sense of urgency. At the forefront was Captain Henry Calloway, his authoritative presence unmistakable as he strode forward, flanked by members of the Boston Board of Health, whose solemn expressions betrayed the gravity of the situation. The Medical Review Committee members closely followed their notepads at the ready, prepared to document every detail.

Among them, Dr. Everett Sinclair, a tall, bespectacled man with an air of intensity, broke away from the group and approached Aldridge directly. His sharp eyes surveyed the scene, taking in the peeling paint on the walls and the flickering fluorescent lights overhead. With a steady voice, he began to question Aldridge, who stood nervously by, acutely aware of the weight of their scrutiny and the mysteries hidden within the asylum walls.

"Your records show extreme treatments."

Aldridge was eerily calm. "My patients require discipline."

Dr. Sinclair narrowed his eyes. "Your work ends today, Dr. Aldridge."

Deep within the dimly lit confines of the asylum's children's ward, Lily lay curled up in the small, metal-framed bed that felt far too big and cold for her tiny frame. The thin, frayed blanket barely offered her any warmth, and her small fingers clutched its edges, as if trying to pull the fabric closer against the chill that seeped into her bones. She was too tired to cry, her eyes heavy with exhaustion from sleepless nights spent listening to the distant echoes of muted whispers and the soft, mournful cries of other lost children.

Then—an unexpected voice broke through the silence, a soft whisper that seemed to carry both comfort and intrigue, pulling her from the depths of her weary thoughts. It felt as if the shadows around her had suddenly taken on life, beckoning her to listen, to understand.

"Lily!"

The moment Lily saw Katie, she gasped in disbelief.

"Katie?"

Katherine dropped to her knees, reaching for her.

"It's me, little one. I'm here."

Lily burst into sobs, launching into her sister's arms. "I thought you left me," she cried. "I was so scared."

Katherine clutched her tightly, whispering into her hair.

"Never. I will never leave you."

Mary-Alice wiped away a tear. "They're finally together."

The carriage stood waiting outside of Ridgefield. Katherine turned, staring at the dark asylum one last time. *This place will never hold me again.* Daniel helped her inside, keeping her close. Elias sat across from them, silent, his expression unreadable.

Mary-Alice held Cassandra's hand, whispering, "You're safe now."

As the carriage moved forward, Ridgefield faded into the distance.

Martha stood at the door of the Taylor Estate, eyes wide as Lily leaped into her arms.

"Oh, my sweet girl! My sweet Lily!"

Inside, Margaret paced restlessly. When Katherine entered, Margaret froze.

"Katherine?"

Then, Nathaniel stepped inside.

His eyes met Margaret's, time halting between them. Margaret's breath shook.

"Oh my God... I've waited so long to see you again."

Nathaniel's throat tightened. "And I've waited for you."

The night air was crisp, carrying the comforting scent of fresh pine mixed with a hint of burning wood from nearby chimneys. Katherine stepped outside, feeling the cool breeze dancing against her skin like a gentle caress. She paused for a moment, her breath visible in the chill, as she took in the star-speckled sky stretching infinitely above her. Daniel followed closely, his gaze locked onto her with an intensity that hinted at emotions concealed just below the surface. The faint glow of the porch light illuminated his features, revealing a mix of admiration and uncertainty in his eyes.

"You saved me," she whispered.

Daniel shook his head. "No, Katherine. You saved yourself."

Her breath caught. No one had ever told her that before. Slowly, his fingers traced the side of her face, hesitant, reverent.

"You don't have to say anything," he murmured.

Katherine didn't.

Instead, she leaned in, closing the space between them with a palpable warmth that filled the air. Daniel's breath hitched, a mixture of surprise and anticipation swirling within him. Slowly, he found himself leaning closer until their lips finally met in a gentle embrace. It wasn't rushed or frantic; there was a tender deliberation to their connection. This kiss was a heartfelt promise, an unspoken agreement that transcended words. As the world around them faded into a soft blur of colors and sounds, Katherine felt an exhilarating wave of freedom wash over her, as if, at that moment, she could finally be herself without fear or hesitation.

Chapter Forty-One: A New Beginning

The bells of St. Augustine's Chapel rang across the city, their chimes echoing through the cobblestone streets of Boston. The crisp March air carried the sound, drawing the attention of onlookers who watched carriages arrive one by one, carrying guests dressed in their finest attire. Adorned with white roses, fresh lilies, and golden candlelight, the church held an air of sacred beauty.

Inside, the warm glow of hundreds of flickering candles reflected off the tall stained-glass windows, painting the wooden pews in hues of sapphire, ruby, and gold. The scent of polished wood and the soft fragrance of Katherine's chosen lilies filled the air. Katherine stood at the church entrance, her heart pounding not with fear but with anticipation. Nathaniel Taylor, dressed in a distinguished black coat and cravat, stood by her side, offering his arm. His expression was one of quiet admiration.

"You have come through so much, my dear," he murmured. "And now, today, you step forward into the life you deserve."

Katherine swallowed the lump in her throat, blinking back the tears that threatened to fall. For so long, she had been trapped in fear, in expectations that were never her own. But this? This was her choice. With a slow breath, she stepped forward.

Daniel Hahn stood tall at the altar, his hands clasped before him. He wore a sharp black frock coat, navy waistcoat, and crisp white shirt. His usually unruly brown hair was neatly combed, and his strong jaw was freshly shaven. But what stole Katherine's breath was how he looked at her as if she were the most beautiful woman he had ever seen. His eyes never wavered, locked onto hers as she approached him.

Father Benedict Callahan, a man of sixty-three with graying hair and a voice rich with wisdom, stood before them, his gold and crimson vestments marking the sacredness of the ceremony. When Katherine reached Daniel's side, he took her hands in his, his thumb brushing over her knuckles. The ceremony began, and Father Callahan's words filled the chapel, speaking of love, devotion, and a bond meant to last a lifetime.

"Daniel Hahn, do you take Katherine Taylor to be your lawful wedded wife, to love, honor, and cherish her, in sickness and health, for as long as you both shall live?"

Daniel's voice was deep and unwavering.

"With all my heart, I do."

Father Callahan turned to Katherine.

"Do you, Katherine Taylor, take Daniel Hahn to be your lawful wedded husband, to love, honor, and cherish him in sickness and health for as long as you both shall live?"

As she whispered, "I do, " tears welled in Katherine's eyes.

As they exchanged rings—a delicate silver band for Katherine and an engraved silver one for Daniel—the warmth of Daniel's touch sent a shiver through her.

Father Callahan smiled warmly. "By the power vested in me, I now pronounce you husband and wife." Daniel wasted no time. He cupped her face and kissed her—deeply as if the entire world had melted away.

The church erupted in heartfelt applause, but neither of them noticed; their world had contracted into a singular, breathtaking moment—this love, fierce and unwavering, this life woven together with dreams and promises.

The reception at Nathaniel's estate was a vibrant tapestry of warmth and joy. The expansive ballroom, once a somber setting for rigid, formal gatherings under Reginald's reign, had been magnificently transformed into a sanctuary of celebration. The grand chandelier overhead spilled a cascade of golden light over the elegantly draped silk tablecloths, shimmering fine china, and a lavish spread of culinary delights that could rival the grandest feasts in Boston. Laughter and music intertwined, creating an atmosphere as radiant as the love being honored.

The room was filled with laughter and music. Violins played a lively waltz as guests twirled across the polished floors. Katherine and Daniel sat side by side at the head table, hands entwined.

Margaret, seated next to Nathaniel, seemed lighter, freer. They spoke in soft, private exchanges, a tenderness growing between them after years of separation. Lily danced barefoot across the ballroom, twirling between Katherine and Daniel, her delighted giggles warming the room. Elias Montgomery stood at the refreshment table, watching the festivities from a quiet distance. Martha was all smiles as she was happy for the beautiful couple and a happy Lily.

Cassandra Jones approached him, offering a small smile. "It's a beautiful evening," she said.

Elias sighed, swirling the drink in his hand. "It is."

He looked at her—honestly, looked at her. She had once been fragile, lost, much like himself. But now, there was strength in her eyes. Perhaps they both had a future beyond the ghosts of Ridgefield.

A week later, Katherine and Daniel settled into their new home, a charming townhouse in Beacon Hill, a gift from Nathaniel. The house had tall windows with flowing curtains, dark mahogany floors, and a grand fireplace in the parlor. It was not the estate she had grown up in, nor was it grand or imposing. It was home. Daniel lifted Katherine into his arms, grinning.

"You are mine now, Mrs. Hahn."

She laughed, wrapping her arms around his neck. "And you, my husband, are mine."

He kissed her again—softly, sweetly, a promise sealed between them.

The courtroom was packed weeks later, buzzing with spectators, officials, and former Ridgefield victims. Dr. Julian Aldridge stood before the judge, his hands neatly folded, his expression eerily calm.

One by one, witnesses took the stand. Mary-Alice spoke first. "Dr. Aldridge did not heal his patients—he broke them."

Katherine's testimony was quiet but firm. "I was sent to Ridgefield for no crime but disobedience to my father. What I endured there will never leave me."

The judge's gavel struck sharply after the jury read the guilty verdict on three criminal charges.

"Dr. Julian Aldridge, you are hereby stripped of your medical license and sentenced to life imprisonment."

As he was led away in chains, Aldridge turned to Katherine with a chilling smirk.

"You look so much like her."

The individual paused momentarily, visibly surprised, and abruptly left the scene.

The Boston Board of Health and the Police Department officially shut down Ridgefield. Captain Henry Calloway and Officer Robert Dean stood at the entrance as the gates were locked for the final time.

"It's over," Dean murmured.

"No," Calloway corrected. "It should have never begun."

Many patients were reunited with their families, but others would need care for the rest of their lives.

The building remained—a ghost of its past.

That evening, as the fire crackled in the hearth, Katherine sat with Lily on the porch of their new home. Lily leaned into her, wrapped in a thick wool shawl.

"Katie?"

Katherine smiled, brushing a curl from her sister's cheek. "Yes, my love?"

"We're safe now, right?"

Katherine held her close.

"Yes, Lily. We are safe. And we are together."

And for the first time in her life, Katherine knew it was true.

Chapter Forty-Two: A Future Reclaimed

The halls of Hawthorne Academy were filled with the laughter and chatter of young girls as Mary-Alice Alexander walked through the courtyard, a woven medical satchel hanging over her arm. The crisp spring air carried the scent of lilac blossoms, and the distant sound of church bells signaled the passing hour.

For the first time in years, Mary-Alice felt at peace. She had spent so long caring for women without hope of escape. Now, she was surrounded by life, by children who still had the chance for a future. As she stepped into the infirmary, she noticed a small figure curled up on the cot near the window. A young girl, no older than nine, with thin arms and tangled chestnut hair, sat silently staring at the floor.

Mary-Alice knelt beside her, speaking gently. "What's your name, sweetheart?"

The girl hesitated before whispering, "Edith."

Mary-Alice gave a soft smile. "You seem troubled, Edith. Would you like to talk?"

The child looked up, her brown eyes filled with a sadness Mary-Alice had seen before—in the eyes of women locked behind Ridgefield's walls.

A child who had been abandoned. A child without a home. A foster child.

Mary-Alice's chest tightened. She had thought she had left Ridgefield behind, but the scars of forgotten children and unwanted souls still haunted the world beyond its gates. I couldn't save them all, she thought. But I can save one. With Edith's hand, she whispered, "No matter what happens, Edith, you are not alone."

The city streets of Boston bustled with activity as Cassandra Jones hurried down Washington Street, dodging pedestrians and horse-drawn carriages. Her hands clutched a stack of ledgers, the weight oddly satisfying. She had never thought she would be here working a real job, living freely in a city that had once felt so out of reach.

The Whitmores, a kind couple who owned the furniture shop, had hired her as their new secretary. She organized orders, managed correspondence, and helped wealthy clients select furniture. It was mundane work—but it was hers. She heard a familiar voice behind her as she stepped into the shop.\"You're late."

Cassandra turned to see Elias Montgomery leaning casually against the counter, his arms crossed.

She smirked. "I am precisely on time."

Elias chuckled, shaking his head. He had been visiting the shop every afternoon, offering to walk her home.

It had started as an excuse. Now, it was routine.

"Come," Elias said, offering his arm. "I know a café that serves the best tea in all of Boston. And I know a woman who deserves something warm after a long work day."

Cassandra hesitated, but only for a moment before taking his arm. She had been afraid too long, waiting for the world to hurt her again. For once, she was choosing happiness.

The Taylor Estate stood in solemn silence, its grand façade casting long shadows in the late afternoon sun. Inside, Nathaniel Taylor sat in his study, pen in hand, a single sheet of paper before him: Reginald Taylor's official death certificate.

Cause of death: Heart Attack.

Nathaniel sighed, tapping the pen against his desk. He knew the truth. Margaret had killed her husband. She had poisoned his tea.

And yet…

Reginald had been a monster. Nathaniel had spent weeks debating what to do. He had interviewed staff, examined records, and listened to Martha's hushed confessions. In the end, he had made his decision. Reginald's death would remain officially recorded as natural. Nathaniel signed his name at the bottom, sealing the truth into silence. He would not let Margaret suffer for doing what needed to be done. And he would not let Reginald's memory haunt his family any longer. Martha watched from the parlor as Nathaniel and Margaret sat together, speaking quietly. For years, she had been the loyal servant of Reginald Taylor, a man who had ruled his household with an iron grip. She had feared him. But Nathaniel was different. Margaret had changed. She had fought for her daughters. She had endured and survived. Martha felt something she had never expected to feel for Margaret Taylor. Respect.

She turned away, allowing them their privacy. Nathaniel reached across the table, taking Margaret's hands in his. His voice was low, filled with something unspoken, something fragile.

"We have lost too many years."

Margaret's breath hitched. "Nathaniel..."

His fingers tightened around hers.

"Let's not waste any more."

Tears welled in Margaret's eyes as she whispered, "Yes."

It was a quiet engagement. A second chance. For both of them.

That evening, the Taylor Estate was filled with the scent of warm bread and fresh tea as Katherine, Daniel, Lily, Nathaniel, Margaret, Elias, and Cassandra gathered in the dining room. For the first time in years, laughter echoed through the halls. Lily sat at Katherine's side, her tiny fingers laced with hers. Nathaniel poured wine, toasting to new beginnings. Margaret smiled softly, no longer burdened by fear. Elias and Cassandra exchanged glances across the table, something new blossoming between them. And Katherine looked around at the faces of those she loved. She had been locked away, betrayed, abandoned. She had lost so much. But now? Now, she was free to love and be loved without consequences.

Epilogue: The Shadows of the Past

One Year Later

The air in Boston was crisp and fresh, the scent of early spring drifting through the Cobblestone streets. Life had continued for everyone, each finding their place in the world after the horrors of Ridgefield. Katherine and Daniel had settled into married life beautifully. Their home in Beacon Hill was filled with warmth and love. Lily had flourished under Katherine's care, her laughter filling the halls as she grew into a bright and joyful young girl.

Nathaniel and Margaret had finally married after months of quiet courtship. They had chosen a private ceremony away from the gossip of high society. Elias and Cassandra had become inseparable. Though Elias still carried some old wounds, Cassandra's presence soothed him in ways he never thought possible. He had stopped drinking so much, focusing instead on rebuilding his family business.

Mary-Alice continued her work at Hawthorne Academy, finding a sense of purpose in helping young girls like Edith, offering them the kindness she wished she could have given the women of Ridgefield.

Everything was peaceful until the news arrived: The Announcement—A New Asylum Rises. Katherine sat in the parlor, reading the morning paper, a soft breeze drifting through the open window. Her tea sat untouched. The moment her eyes landed on the article, her breath caught in her throat. Her hands trembled as she scanned the words. "With the closing of Ridgefield Asylum, the need for a proper facility has been evident. Dr. Dennis Evans, a respected psychiatrist from New York, has moved to Boston to open Briarwood Sanitarium, promising humane treatment and innovative psychiatric care... Katherine's heart pounded. She could hardly breathe. She stood abruptly, the newspaper slipping from her grasp, the inked words blurring before her eyes. A new asylum. A new prison for women like her. For women who would not be believed. She staggered back, her vision spinning.

"Katie?"

Lily stood in the doorway, her small face etched with worry. Katherine smiled, though her chest felt like it was caving in.

"It's nothing, my love. Go play."

But it wasn't nothing. Not to the women who would suffer. Not to the ghosts of Ridgefield. That night, Katherine woke up screaming. The walls of Ridgefield surrounded her. Dr. Aldridge loomed over her, his hands tightening the restraints. The cold metal table bit into her skin. She struggled, fighting against the restraints holding her down.

A voice whispered in her ear, low and cold— "You look so much like her."

She thrashed, trying to scream, but the sound never came.

Dr. Aldridge kissed Katherine's forehead.

"Dear mother, you sinned."

Dr. Aldridge turned on the electroconvulsive therapy machine, and Katherine convulsed against the restraints.

Made in the USA
Columbia, SC
25 March 2025